Charles Godfrey Leland
and His Magical Tales

Praise for
Charles Godfrey Leland and His Magical Tales

"With *Charles Godfrey Leland and His Magical Tales*, Jack Zipes brings attention to the too often neglected work of a nineteenth- and early twentieth-century amateur and intellectual omnivore. Leland was an amateur because he was not employed as an academic and also because (like Zipes himself) he was driven by a love of the subjects he researched. This anthology gathers a selection of great potential interest to historians and anthropologists as well as to fairy-tale scholars."

—Pauline Greenhill, professor of women's and gender studies,
University of Winnipeg, Manitoba, Canada

"Reading *Charles Godfrey Leland and His Magical Tales* is quite a trip! Meet a cannibal Chenoo transformed into family by a woman's kindness, the Cinderella-like bride of the Invisible One, a virtuous woman turned into a fly with silver wings, a fairy walking the streets of Florence in the shape of a girl, Virgil and Merlin—both great wizards, more than one magic key, and many 'false truths and true lies.' Whether retelling Native American, Italian, or Romani tales, Leland creates vivid mini-worlds ruled by transformation, the wheels of fortune, and magic. As editor, Jack Zipes does not attempt to rein in Leland's imagination. Instead, he cautions us to recognize his appropriative lens as 'amateur folklorist' and invites us to appreciate his gusto for storytelling."

—Cristina Bacchilega, University of Hawaiʻi at Mānoa

"The best fairy tales of Charles Godfrey Leland are gathered here, subtly burnished by Jack Zipes. Algonquin tales of magic include a fascinating Micmac variant of Cinderella; in stories of an enchanted Italy a girl may be transformed into a cow or a fly, and Virgil stars as a mighty sorcerer."

—Neil Philip, author of *The Penguin Book of English Folktales*

"Charles Godfrey Leland remains one of the most brilliant and unjustly neglected nineteenth-century American folklorists. His extraordinary range was unified by a passionate commitment to natural wisdom—from Canadian Algonquins to English Romani to the surviving traditions of Tuscan witchcraft. This stunning collection brings to light a forgotten monument of folkloric literature."

—Joseph Sobol, director, George Ewart Evans Centre for Storytelling,
University of South Wales

Charles Godfrey Leland and His Magical Tales

Edited by
Jack Zipes

Wayne State University Press
Detroit

Series in Fairy-Tale Studies

Series Editor

Donald Haase, Wayne State University

A complete listing of the advisory editors and the books in this series can be found online at wsupress.wayne.edu.

ISBN 978-0-8143-4785-0 (paperback)
ISBN 978-0-8143-4786-7 (hardcover)
ISBN 978-0-8143-4787-4 (e-book)

Library of Congress Control Number: 2020938183

The images for the cover and interior feature woodcut prints created by Jack Zipes. The frontispiece and cover image was inspired by a photograph of Charles Godfrey Leland in Elizabeth Robins Pennell's biography *Charles Godfrey Leland*, vol. 1 (Boston: Archibald Constable, 1904).

Published with the assistance of a fund established by Thelma Gray James of Wayne State University for the publication of folklore and English studies.

Wayne State University Press
Leonard N. Simons Building
4809 Woodward Avenue
Detroit, Michigan 48201-1309

Visit us online at wsupress.wayne.edu

Contents

The Unpublished Legends of Virgil

Romani Tales

Introduction

The Many Voices and Lives of
Charles Godfrey Leland

Jack Zipes

IT IS VIRTUALLY IMPOSSIBLE to assess Charles Godfrey Leland and his significance for American and European culture because he had so many diverse identities in different contexts and often all at one time—disgruntled Princeton student, awestruck scholar in Germany, combatant in the 1848 French Revolution, journalist, humorist, translator, soldier in the Northern Army during the Civil War, speculator, dilettante folklorist, researcher of customs and lore of Native Americans, British Romani, and African Americans, protofeminist, founder of industrial art schools in Philadelphia, and pioneer in the studies of magic, which he took most seriously. He was also charismatic, hyperbolic, opportunistic, and a "devout" believer in the power of nature and magic. For Leland, all truths can be discovered in nature by learning the secrets of magic and shamanism. This is why he himself constantly shape-shifted and drew close to marginalized people.

How could one person have assumed so many different roles and identities in his lifetime, as well as in the societies in which he worked and thrived? Clearly, Leland had a monstrous curiosity and appetite to explore everything with which he came into contact. Naïve and worldly, there was nothing he really knew thoroughly as a specialist. Yet, he always wanted to know more than other specialist researchers did.

Toward the end of his career, the *New York Tribune* published the following tribute to Leland:

The recent publication by Mr. Charles Godfrey Leland of a volume of Florentine legends provokes a comment not strictly related to the book in question. It is intrinsically valuable, but it sets one thinking also of what notable services Mr. Leland has rendered to literature, to the study of folklore, to industrial art, to more interests than can be touched upon here. It inspires some wonder as to why we hear so little of him, as to why nothing seems to be getting itself done in the preparation of a complete and uniform edition of his works, beginning with Hans Breitmann and embracing all his multifarious essays in fascinating fields. The list is divided among several publishers, and while specialists laud this book and that, there is no concentrated recognition of Mr. Leland's significance as a man of letters.[1]

The present collection of his tales is not intended to be a "complete and uniform edition of his works." Given their quantity and diversity, that would be, in my opinion, impossible. Instead, to give readers an idea of his extraordinary research, I have selected and edited representative folk- and fairy tales, legends, and stories from five books that he published in the period 1873–1901: *The Gypsies* (1882), *The Algonquin Legends of New England* (1884), *Gypsy Sorcery and Fortune-Telling* (1891), *Legends of Florence*, two volumes (1895–96), and *The Unpublished Legends of Virgil* (1901). Though these tales cannot be considered "authentic" folktales, that is, stories taken down word by word from the lips of Romani, Native Americans, real witches, peasants, and folklorists, they are highly significant because of their historical and cultural value.

In most instances, Leland recorded these tales by hand in personal encounters with his informants, or he collected them from friends and acquaintances. He then honed the tales for publication so that they became translations of the narratives, not exactly the same as those he heard or

---

1. *New York Tribune*, July 28, 1895, Box 371, Pennell-Whistler Collection, Library of Congress, Washington, DC.

received. This is not to say that he made major changes. But the fact of the matter is that he was like most of the aspiring American folklorists of his time, 1850 to 1900, who were mainly white, male, and from the middle classes. The foremost American collectors such as Franz Boas, George Lyman Kittredge, Thomas Crane, Francis James Child, and many others were dedicated to a project of preserving the culture of minority groups and societies in America and foreign countries. In America and Europe, highly educated, independent, and literate scholars took a great interest in various groups of people who allegedly could not speak or write for themselves and yet were historically vital for understanding the civilizing process of the dominant and elite groups. What distinguishes Leland from the major folklorists of the nineteenth century is his *literary* bent. All the tales, no matter whether they were from Romani, Native Americans, witches, or colleagues, were transformed and often embellished by Leland to represent his particular regard for their poetry, purity, and history. Embedded were secrets that were truths, and in this regard, Leland was a seeker of truth.

In the early part of the nineteenth century, most American folklorists were originally not associated with a university, and the field of folklore had not yet been established as a "legitimate" discipline in the academy. The American Folklore Society was first founded in 1888, and the members endeavored to set standards for collecting and publishing tales that evolved out of a productive schism. In Rosemary Lévy Zumwalt's superb book, *American Folklore Scholarship: A Dialogue of Dissent*, she examines how the literary folklorists tended to be more concerned with texts, whereas the anthropologists focused on the context and the life of the people. Both groups had the same goal: to establish folklore as a legitimate science or field of study in the American academy.

Leland was untrained as a folklorist and did not play a major role in the American Folklore Society, or in England, because he traveled a great deal. Aware of the schism, he nevertheless did not take sides, for he was an adherent of both. In fact, he was very independent and often did his work through a love for the esoteric and the customs and beliefs of indigenous people. He never conformed to the rules and regulations of either group. His major contribution to the new field of folklore was his exploration of magic and shamanism. Leland wanted to be something other than he was, and by studying the lore and customs of dominated groups, he sought to become part of these groups and to "cleanse" himself of civilizing forces. Here I think that Angela-Marie Varesano summarizes his position best:

> Folklore was for him, during the 1880's, an activity that enabled him to become close to Nature and to apprehend the sublime poetry within it. It brought him into the woods, and semi-wilds, where he came into contact with people who lived close to Nature, with Nature's children and mediators. Folklore included those strange narratives of legends and beliefs that were in themselves a kind of poetry. Indeed, Leland asserts that most of these Indian traditions were originally poems, and that it is probably that all were sung, while they still retained the character of serious mythical or sacred narrative, although when he found them, they were in a transition state of heroic tales. He conceived of his job as a collector to be that of an interpreter as well; thus, he felt it was necessary to compile the fragments, versions, and episodes of adventures available to him into a whole that had dramatic impact on the reader. He was concerned that the material presented in his books spoke not to the admirer of precisely-recorded words, but to those who could appreciate the poetry within them.[2]

Born on August 15, 1824, in Philadelphia to a prosperous merchant's family, Charles Godfrey Leland was expected to follow in his father's footsteps and become a lawyer or businessman. However, as a young boy, who was often sick, he attended several different schools and showed more interest in the occult, philosophy, and literature. Consequently, it was clear that his "destiny" would have little to do with commerce or law. Soon after he passed his Latin examinations in high school, he was accepted to study at

---

2. Angela-Marie Joanna Varesano, "Charles Godfrey Leland: The Eclectic Folklorist" (PhD diss., University of Pennsylvania, 1979), 13.

Princeton University, where he continued his exploration of Gnosticism and metaphysics and wrote stories and poems until his graduation in 1845. Since he did not show an affinity for any particular profession, his father suggested that he join one of his cousins and study for a year or two in Europe. This was a turning point in his life.

Leland had never shown any interest in politics, and at this time in Europe, in almost every country he visited before the 1848 revolutions, the political tensions were strong, and he was often drawn into conversations about slavery in America, civil rights, and government. In his *Memoirs*, he wrote, "I had never thought much of this subject before I left home. I did not *like* slavery, nor to think about it. But in Europe I did like such thought, and I returned fully impressed with the belief that slavery was, as Charles Sumner said, 'the sum of all crimes.'"[3] In short, his studies in Germany and France and his trips to other countries such as Austria and Italy contributed to an awakening of social inequities and injustice. It is important to remember that he was only twenty-one and a gangly six-foot-two naïve American when he left for Europe and that he had never really lived on his own. Aside from learning about different cultural differences on the Continent, he began enjoying drinking at taverns and debating, and for a young man raised in a Quaker city by Unitarian/Episcopalian parents, this was a major step toward independent thinking and acting. Eventually, it led to his fighting on the barricades in Paris against the royalists.

It would be misleading, however, to think that Leland became a left-wing rebel or broke with the legacy of his family. As his letters to his parents and younger brother Henry show, Leland was very devoted to his mother and father and grateful to them for giving him the opportunity to spend three years in Europe.[4] When he returned home, he showed his appreciation by studying law to assist his father. However, this gesture was short-lived, and Leland spent the next ten years working as an editor and journalist for various magazines and newspapers in Philadelphia and New York City.

---

3. Charles Godfrey Leland, *Memoirs*, vol. 1 (London: William Heinemann, 1893), 190.
4. This correspondence is largely in the Library of Congress, Washington, DC.

In 1849, he met his future wife, Isabelle Fisher, who was from a notable Philadelphian family, and he married her in 1855. She was to remain his loyal wife for the rest of his peripatetic life, and it is unfortunate that we do not have records of her life because she must have been remarkably strong and brave to have put up with the ever-wandering Leland. During this period he was somewhat stable and moved to New York, where he began a real apprenticeship as editor for various publications; he wrote hundreds of articles on opera, the theater, literature, politics, and philosophy and began publishing popular books such as *The Poetry and Mystery of Dreams* (1856) and *Meister Karl's Sketch-Book* (1855) and translated Heinrich Heine's *Pictures of Travel and Book Songs* (1855), which received excellent reviews.

When he did not find a permanent job in New York, he returned to Philadelphia and continued writing and editing magazines and newspapers. However, his literary activities came to a full stop in 1862 when the Civil War erupted; he and his younger brother Henry joined the army of the North in 1864 as privates and fought for the abolition of slavery until the end of 1865. Unfortunately, Henry, with whom Leland was very close, was wounded at one point and eventually died from his injuries in 1869.

After the Civil War ended, Leland was unemployed and spent a year in his father's house, again writing for various newspapers and journals and pondering his next step, for he still did not feel "grounded" in any particular job. All he wanted to do was to write while his father proclaimed him a failure and ne'er do well.[5] Unfortunately, his father never lived long enough to see how his son became famous, in not only America but also Europe after the publication of his popular book, *Hans Breitmann's Ballads* (1868). His father died the very same year.

For over ten years, Leland had been publishing amusing ditties in his own invented German-American dialect about a fictitious immigrant named Hans Breitmann, who comes to America after the 1848 Revolution

---

5. "My father regarded me as a failure in life, or as a literary ne'er-do-weel, destined never to achieve fortune or gain an état, and he was quite right. My war experience had made me reckless of life, and speculation was firing every heart." Leland, *Memoirs*, 2:76.

failed and tries to find a new home and role in life. Leland's famous first ballad begins this way:

Hans Breitmann's Party

Hans Breitmann gife a barty,
Dey had biano-blayin;
I felled in lofe mit a Merican frau,
Her name vas Madilda Yane.
She hat haar as prown ash a pretzel,
Her eyes vas himmel-plue,
Und ven dey looket indo mine,
Dey shplit mine heart in two.

Hans Breitmann gife a barty,
I vent dere you'll pe pound.
I valtzet mit Madilda Yane
Und vent shpinnen round und round.
De pootiest Fraeulein in de House,
She vayed 'pout dwo hoondred pound,
Und efery dime she gife a shoomp
She made de vindows sound.[6]

The good-hearted, beer-drinking, courageous Breitmann was never a figure of satire. Rather, Leland, who admired Germans and German culture, wanted to depict how difficult it was for Germans (and perhaps other immigrants) to adapt to American culture during a period of civil unrest. The humor of the ballads, often sent in letters to friends, was intended to provide relief in hard times. And it was relief that Leland and his wife were seeking when they decided to use his father's inheritance and earnings from

---

6. Charles Godfrey Leland, *Hans Breitmann's Party with Other Ballads* (Philadelphia: T. B. Peterson & Brothers, 1868), 5. The best complete edition is *Hans Breitmann's Ballads* (Boston: Houghton Mifflin, 1914) with an introduction by Elizabeth Robins Pennell, Leland's niece, and with a preface by Leland.

his writings to live abroad for a few years. In the meantime, *Hans Breit-mann's Ballads* was a huge success in America, and this was also the case in England. As Elizabeth Robins Pennell, Leland's niece and biographer, wrote: "Breitmann's success was scarcely less in England, where he came and conquered almost as soon as at home, though it is hard to say just why the *Ballads* with their curious medley of what their author describes as 'Teutonic philosophy and sentiment, beer, music and romance,' should have appealed to the British public. . . . Everybody wanted to read Breitmann and, when the author of Breitmann arrived in England, everybody wanted to see Breitmann. He was the lion of London drawing-rooms as long as he could endure the discomfort of it."[7]

Indeed, England was so receptive and intriguing for the Lelands that they remained there a good eleven years, and it was during this time that Leland turned away from drawing rooms to embrace the English Romani. Leland did not have any set plans when he and his wife arrived in England, and they spent 1870 touring the country. After settling down in London, he and his wife took a trip to Brighton with friends to visit the ruins of an ancient Roman fort. While there, they had an encounter which was to influence all his future work and enabled him to change his identity as the author of the Breitmann ballads to that of a dedicated folklorist. As he wrote about his visit to Brighton in his *Memoirs*:

> The living curiosity of the place was a famous old gypsy woman named Gentilla Cooper, a pure blood or real *Kalorat* Romany. I had already in America studied Pott's "Thesaurus of Gypsy Dialects," and picked up many phrases of the tongue from the works of Borrow, Simson and others. The old dame tackled us at once. As soon as I could, I whispered in her ear an impro-vised rhyme:—"The basho and kani, / The rye and the rani, Hav'd akai 'pre' o boro lon pani." Which means that the cock and the hen, the gentleman and the lady, came hither across

7. Elizabeth Robins Pennell, introduction to *Hans Breitmann's Ballads* (Boston: Houghton Mifflin, 1914), x–xi.

the great salt water. The effect on the gypsy was startling; she fairly turned pale. Hustling the ladies away to one side to see a beautiful view, she got me alone and hurriedly exclaimed, "Rya—master! *be* you one of our people?" with much more. We became very good friends, and this little incident had in time for me great results, and many strange experiences of gypsy life.[8]

Angela-Marie Varesano points out in "Charles Godfrey Leland: The Eclectic Folklorist" that Leland's future method of collecting of tales from indigenous people whether in America or in Europe depended on the serendipitous meeting of unusual people who would help him discover legends, wonder tales, animal tales, and secrets about magic that he would then record and shape for publication. Moreover, Leland would always try to impress his informants by speaking in their language or demonstrating knowledge of their culture.

In the case of the English Romani, he became so enraptured by their customs, songs, and stories that he learned the Romany language as best he could and transformed himself into the Rey, which meant respected gentleman, a title and identity that he loved to assume until his death in 1903. In 1873 Leland published *The English Gipsies and Their Language*, which included folk stories, customs, sayings, and songs collected directly from the mouths of the Romani. However, Leland typically embellished and reworked all his narratives while remaining true to his intention to portray humble people. There is some hubris to his method, and consequently, while his tales are lively renditions of Romany anecdotes and customs, they are his interpretations and reflect his particular approach to all the materials he gathered from "natural" people whom he admired. Varesano perceptively comments: "The study of the Gypsy, for Leland, was in a very real way the study of Nature itself. These strange people were for him a contact with that well-spring of all art and truth which he praised. The Gypsies were fascinating and important because they were a people still in contact with nature,

---

8. Leland, *Memoirs*, 2:407.

and in learning their ways, in studying them, in becoming one of them, he was participating in the truest kind of art. This idea will be found in all his subsequent studies of folklore; it underlies his fieldwork with the American Indians, and the investigation of the sorceresses of Italy."[9]

From 1871 until his return to Philadelphia in 1879, Leland took many different trips in North Africa and Europe, and wherever he went, he continued to study and learn Romani dialects and customs to preserve vanishing relics of ancient times. Two important results of his research and travels were *English Gypsy Songs* (1875) and *The Gypsies* (1882). However, it was not just the Romani who enabled him to develop and cultivate his folkloristic philosophy but also his later studies of the American Indians, the Etruscans, and the magic of Italian witches. For Leland, it was impossible to understand present living conditions without fully understanding the past. As he stated later in *Gypsy Sorcery and Fortune-Telling*, "There is nothing whatever in the past relating to the influences which have swayed man, however strange, eccentric, superstitious, or even repulsive they may seem, which is not of great and constantly increasing value. And if we of the present time begin already to see this, how much more important will these facts be to the men of the future, who, by virtue of more widely extended knowledge and comparison, will be better able than we are to draw wise conclusions undreamed of now. But the chief conclusion for us is to *collect* as much as we can, while it is yet extant, of all the strange lore of the olden time, instead of wasting time in forming idle theories about it."[10]

Although Leland and his wife had established themselves in London, and Leland himself had become a recognized authority of Romani life in England, they suddenly decided to return to Philadelphia in 1879. Always curious and active, Leland, who had been a very good artist and designer, began to take a strong interest in the teaching of industrial arts, and he spent the next four years teaching at the Industrial Art School in Philadelphia, which he helped to establish. Obviously influenced by the Arts and Crafts

---

9. Varesano, "Charles Godfrey Leland," 94.

10. Charles Godfrey Leland, *Gypsy Sorcery and Fortune-Telling* (London: T. Fisher Unwin, 1891), ix.

movement in England, Leland believed that public schools should cater to the interests of young people from the lower classes who needed technical and art training so that they could learn a trade. Up to that point, there were no schools in Philadelphia that provided the children of disadvantaged families with such an education. At the same time he was teaching, he went on to publish several books such as *The Minor Arts* (1879), *Practical Education* (1888), and *Drawing and Designing* (1889) to disseminate his ideas. In 1892, he designed one of his own books, *The Book of One Hundred Riddles of the Fairy Bellaria* (1892), which demonstrates his unusual talent as an artist.[11]

Aside from his major work in public schools, Leland began focusing on American folklore. In the summer of 1882, he was visiting relatives and friends in New England when he met several acculturated Algonquin Indians. While there, he interviewed them and continued to correspond with them for two years. The result from his collaboration with these informants led to the publication of *The Algonquin Legends of New England* (1884), a pamphlet with the title *The Mythology, Legends and Folk-Lore of the Algonkins* (1887), and *Kulóskap the Master and Other Algonkin Poems* (1902). As he had done with the English Romani, Leland sought to celebrate the American Indians as "noble savages," and to a certain extent, this resulted in stereotyping and transforming the Algonquin tales to reflect his own political concerns about America.

In Thomas Parkhill's excellent study, *Weaving Ourselves into the Land: Charles Godfrey Leland, "Indians," and the Study of Native American Religions*, he carefully demonstrates that Leland had racist notions about Native Americans as a young man, but through greater contact with them over the years, his attitudes changed to the point that he admired and celebrated their customs and stories. Moreover, Parkhill maintains that Leland had once again conceived himself as someone else, as part Native American through his contact with the Algonquins, and consequently felt he could

---

11. See the recent reproduction, Charles Godfrey Leland, *The Book of One Hundred Riddles of the Fairy Bellaria*, ed. Jack Zipes (Minneapolis: University of Minnesota Press, 2018).

alter and edit the tales he collected to enable white Americans to understand the profound significance of the tales. Leland believed that the Algonquin tales could reveal that humankind's first religion was shamanism embedded in the magic of the stories. They contained truths that had to be mined. In this regard, he was somewhat of a pioneer and opened the way for other anthropologists such as Franz Boas, who took the magic and shamanism of indigenous people more seriously than they ever had been.

Unlike his writing on the Romani, Leland's collecting of Algonquin legends and stories assumed a "religious" mission. Through understanding the secrets of the Algonquin narratives, Leland hoped his readers would grasp the poetry of nature that made life worth living.[12] Therefore, he focused on the magic of shamanism in the tales and endeavored to give the indigenous people of America a sense of their place in world history. As Parkhill remarks:

> The wild and strong are connected with the "Indian" and the "Indian" with the heart and soul of the United States. Leland, taking that characteristic of the stereotype that vouchsafed the "Indian" was close to nature, employed it in an approving manner in order to meld the tenets of German Romanticism into the unsettled milieu of the Gilded Age of the United States. His aim: to protect the country's heart and soul, to see it "reopened with the fairies of yore," to call Place into being. His efforts to shape, edit, and finally improvise Abenaki and Micmac stories are about making meaning; and not Abenaki or Micmac meaning. They shore up the last part of his story. Leland's anticipation that the nation would come to forge a connection to the natural landscape it had come to inhabit through the vehicle of "Indian" stories is essentially a concern of Place.[13]

---

12. See Thomas Parkhill, *Weaving Ourselves into the Land: Charles Godfrey Leland, "Indians," and the Study of Native American Religions* (Albany: State University of New York Press, 1979), 89–108.

13. Ibid., 101.

As I have emphasized, Leland's approach to folklore and especially indigenous lore was highly unusual at that time. We must remember that the British Folklore Society had just been established in 1878, and the American Folklore Society officially in 1888. Whatever standards were being set for collecting and translating tales were flexible, and even when some were firmly set, they did not apply to Leland. In many ways, he was unique and remained unique as a folklorist until his death. Indeed, he was well aware of his role and made this clear in a letter to his niece in 1895: "There is a great difference between collecting folk-lore as a curiosity and *living* it in truth. I do not believe that in all the Folk-Lore Societies there is one person who lives it in reality as I do. I cannot describe it—what it *once* was is lost to the world. You cannot understand it at second hand."[14]

By June 1884, Leland and his wife decided to return to London, where he hoped to continue his work in the minor arts that was successful in Philadelphia. For the next four years Leland traveled a great deal on the Continent, where he was either writing about the Romani or helping educators in different countries to establish schools based on his books *Practical Education* (1888) and *Drawing and Designing* (1889). In the winter of 1889, the Lelands stopped in Florence, which, unknown to them, was to become their home for the rest of their lives. In fact, it seemed that Leland was destined to live out his life in Florence where he produced, in my opinion, the most intriguing books of his life: *Etruscan Roman Remains in Popular Tradition* (1892), *The Book of One Hundred Riddles of the Fairy Bellaria* (1892), *Legends of Florence* (1895–96), *Aradia; or, The Gospel of the Witches* (1899), and *The Unpublished Legends of Virgil* (1901).

It was in Florence while Leland was wandering the streets one day that he accidentally encountered a young woman by the name of Maddalena, who was going to not only enchant him but also provide him with the information and tales that he published from 1892 until 1902. In his manuscript notes, he describes her as "a young woman who would have been taken for a gypsy in England, but in whose face, in Italy, I soon learned to know

---

14. Elizabeth Robins Pennell, *Charles Godfrey Leland: A Biography* (Boston: Houghton Mifflin, 1906), 2:379.

the antique Etruscan, with its strange mysteries, to which was added the indefinable glance of the Witch. She was from the Romagna Toscana, born in the heart of its unsurpassingly wild and romantic scenery, amid cliffs, headlong torrents, forests and old legendary castles. I did not gather all the facts for a long time, but gradually found that she was of a witch family, or one whose members had, from time immemorial, told fortunes, repeated ancient legends, gathered incantations and learned how to intone them, prepared enchanted medicines, philtres, or spells."[15]

Not only did Maddalena provide him with an abundance of tales, legends, incantations, songs, and spells, but she also introduced Leland to other Italian witches or knowledgeable people who gave him tales and information. Leland saw her constantly while he was living in Florence, and she certainly was the inspiration behind the two volumes of Florentine tales he published in 1895–96. He also credited Marietta Pery, Roma Lister, and Teresa Wyndham for helping him and stated: "My tales are, with a few exceptions, derived directly or indirectly from the people themselves—having been recorded in the local dialect—the exceptions being a few anecdotes racy of the soil taken from antique jest-books and such bygone halfpenny literature as belonged to the multitude, and had its origin among them. These I could not, indeed, well omit, as they refer to some peculiar place in Florence."[16] Leland stresses that all the tales are more or less witch stories because the witches in Italy are the repositories of all the Italian folklore.

His high regard for witches and sorcerers culminated in his fascinating collection of one hundred tales he collected largely from Maddalena about Virgil, not as poet but as a powerful magician. Encouraged by the great Italian scholar Domenico Comparetti, whose book *Vergil in the Middle Ages*[17] is still considered the foremost study of why and how all sorts of tales circulated about Virgil as sorcerer, Leland rewrote forty-six diverse and entertaining

---

15. Ibid., 309–10.
16. Charles Godfrey Leland, *Legends of Florence, Collected from the People and Retold* (London: David Nutt, 1895), vi.
17. See Domenico Comparetti, *Vergil in the Middle Ages*, trans. E. F. M. Benecke, intro. Jan M. Ziolkowski (Princeton: Princeton University Press, 1997).

tales that portray Virgil as a benevolent and wise man who uses his powers to help downtrodden people and defeat evil sorcerers and kings. Some of the tales are ironic and humorous, especially those in which Virgil teaches the emperor of Rome a lesson or two. There was definitely a part of Leland that identified with Virgil and another part, with people on the margins. In the introduction to his book, he wrote:

> One good reason why I obtained so many of these tales so readily is that they were gathered, like my *Florentine Legends* and *Etrusco-Roman Remains*, chiefly among witches or fortune tellers, who, above all other people, preserve with very natural interest all that smacks of sorcery. It is the case in every country—among Red Indians, Hindus or Italians—that wherever there are families in which witchcraft is handed down from generation to generation there will be traditional tales in abundance, and those not of the common fairy-tale kind, but of a mysterious, marvelous nature.[18]

As I have indicated, the tales in the present book have been selected from five different books, *The Algonquin Legends of New England*, *Legends of Florence*, *The Unpublished Legends of Virgil*, *The Gypsies*, and *Gypsy Sorcery and Fortune-Telling*, not in chronological order, because I feel that the first three books on this list are more closely connected and because the pungent Romani tales have little to do with Leland's shamanism and more to do with his picaresque side. Magic and transformation are key to understanding Leland's reworking of the Native American and Italian tales and his reverence for the storytellers, not that he did not revere the Romani. But it is clear that the magical tales of Native Americans and witches were related to a profound philosophical if not religious belief in the poetry and power of nature.

---

18. Charles Godfrey Leland, *The Unpublished Legends of Virgil* (London: Eliot Stock, 1901), xiii.

Today, if Leland and his works are known at all in America, it is mainly by people interested in witchcraft and witchlore. Some even consider him one of the founders of serious witchcraft studies. His book *Aradia; or, The Gospel of the Witches* (1899) had a huge impact on the Wiccan movement[19] and remains a significant resource for contemporary witches, especially since Leland himself took witches and shamanism so seriously.

Would Leland, who often resembled a chameleon and assumed so many different identities, have been happy about his renown mainly among followers of witchcraft? Would he have been sad and insulted that his folklore studies have received such great neglect? There is really no need to speculate because he led a full and meaningful life, and he left us with a range of folktales that are historically unique just as the man himself was—unique.

A Note on the Text

To make the tales in this book more accessible for contemporary readers, I have edited and altered them very carefully. Leland had a tendency to use "thee" and "thou," and his grammar and style are somewhat anachronistic. Though he endeavored to stay close to the oral tradition, his language (expressions and idioms) was very much representative of standard, educated American English of the late nineteenth century. Leland did not try to imitate any of his informants. Rather, he would insert foreign words and expressions into his lively English to provide color to his adapted stories. Leland liked to show off his command of history and languages, and sometimes he can be too didactic. On the other hand, he was, in fact, remarkably knowledgeable and forged an approach to collecting oral tales that few Americans had done at the end of the nineteenth century. We must remember, Leland lived many of these stories. He was absorbed by magical

---

19. See Charles G. Leland, *Aradia; or, The Gospel of the Witches: A New Translation* by Mario Pazzaglini and Dina Pazzaglini with additional material by Chas S. Clifton, Robert Mathiesen, and Robert E. Chartowich, foreword by Stewart Farrar (Blaine, WA: Phoenix, 1998).

tales and storytellers, and there is a wealth of unusual customs and rituals embedded in the tales and his commentaries.

In making changes, I have tried to respect his unique style and have not changed the original meanings of the tales. In some respects, I have interpreted and honed the tales as Leland himself might have done. Often he provided wordy comments to all the tales in his books, and I have only included those comments pertinent to the sociohistorical context of his time. To distinguish between Leland's comments and mine, I have used his initials, CGL, and mine, JZ, in the footnotes. In addition, I want to point out that Leland referred to Romani people as "gypsies" and Native Americans as "Indians" throughout all his works. This was common usage in his day, and he did not mean to disrespect the Romani and Native Americans.

Since there was never an "order" to his tales, I have felt free to choose and select ones that I thought would interest contemporary readers. In many ways, Leland wanted to dignify research into shamanism, magic, and belief systems of common people. His work on Native American and Etruscan lore is groundbreaking. He was not alone in preparing the way for anthropologists to explore the occult, but he was certainly devoted to understanding minority groups and their customs. This is one of the major reasons that I have chosen to try to revive interest in his tales.

Algonquin Tales

The Acquisition of Magic

THERE WERE TWO INDIAN families camped away at some distance from the main village.[1] A young man lived in one of the wigwams, and every night he would go to the other wigwams to see some girls. His mother warned him that he would soon come to harm, for there was danger abroad, but he never minded her.

Now, one night at the end of winter, when the ground was bare of snow, he heard something come after him as he was walking along. It made a very heavy, steady sound. He stopped and saw a long white figure, but without arms or legs. It looked like a corpse all rolled up. The young man was horribly frightened, but when this atrocious ghost-like creature attacked him, he grew angry. Though it had no arms, the creature fought madly. It wrapped itself around him. It struck itself against him and thrashed itself, bending like a fish. And he, too, fought as if he were crazy. He was one of those whose blood and courage go up, but never down. He might die, but he'd never give in until dead. Before daylight the Ghost suggested a rest, or peace. However, the Indian would not hear of it and continued fighting. The Ghost began to beg for mercy, but just then, the youth saw the day break in the north. Then he knew that, if he could but endure the battle a little longer, he would indeed be victorious.

Then the Ghost implored him. "Let me go," he said, "and whatever you may want, you will have, and you'll also have good luck your entire life."

---

1. The first two tales, "The Acquisition of Magic" and "The Golden Key," did not have titles in Leland's book and are taken from the section "Tales of Magic," or *M'téoulin, or Indian Magic*. Tomah Josephs told "The Acquisition of Magic" to Leland to explain how magic (*m'téoulin*) is acquired. [JZ]

Despite all this, the Indian would not yield, for he knew that by conquering he would win all the Ghost had to give. And, as the first ray of the sun shone on him, he became unconscious, and when he awoke, it was as if from a sleep. By his side lay a large, decayed old log, covered with moss. He remembered that, during the fight, he had seemed once to plunge his fist completely into the enemy up to his elbow, and there was a hole in it corresponding to this wound. He had torn away the other's scalp-lock, stripping the skin down to the waist. He found a long, hairy-looking piece of moss ripped from the end of the log to the middle. Pieces of moss and locks of his own hair lay all about him, testifying to the fury of the fight. Indeed, he was terribly bruised and wounded, but he did not pay any attention to this, for now he was another man, and a terrible one.

His mother said, "I warned you of danger."

But he had conquered the danger. He had all the strength of five strong men, and all the power and magic of the Ghost. Yes, the Ghost's spirit itself was now in him. After this, he could do anything and find game where no one else could. To conquer a ghost gives power.[2]

---

2. To conquer the dead, or to fight terrible spirits, to thereby absorb their power, and finally to keep them in a struggle until the day shines on them, is both Norse and Celtic, if not, indeed, world-wide. Clearly, the grim Spirit of this narrative is Norse. This is what the hero possesses as he wrests the sword of victory from a corpse's hold. The great element or chief cause of magic power among the Indians is that of will. It manifests itself in many forms, mere courage being one. Thus, the *Weewillmekq'* confers supernatural ability or other favors but only on those who are not afraid of it. The demon log, as we have just seen, gives strength and prosperity to a man for simply fighting like a bull-dog. Beyond courage, pluck or patience this is what is with these Indians, so closely tied to magic as poetry like the Greeks, or an Eschenwaya. When the true magician "gets mad" and continues to get madder until the end, he is invincible. [CGL]

The Golden Key

(Passamaquoddy)

FAR IN THE WOODS was an Indian town. Near it lived two old people, who had two beautiful daughters, and no son. The girls were very shy. They seldom let themselves be seen. They would not listen to the young men.

The chief of the tribe had a fine son, a great hunter and skilled in mysteries.[1] The young man wanted one of the girls. His father went to their parents and obtained their consent, but the girls refused to be married.

Now, there lived in the village a young man who was neither strong, nor handsome, nor clever at any kind of work. Hearing that the chief's son had failed to get one of the shy or proud girls, he said—but all in jest, for he had but a poor opinion of himself—that he was the right kind of a man to get them. "If they had, for example, only seen *me*, now," he exclaimed, "they would have wished to be married at once!"

Then all who heard him laughed and proposed that they should go that night and try to see the girls and how they might receive the plain-looking youth. So, they went quietly, about supper time, and entered so suddenly that the girls had no time to hide behind the curtain, and thus were obliged to receive the visitors. After supper, they began playing *Mingwadokadjik*. In this game a ring is hidden in the ashes or sand, and each player, with a pointed stick, makes a plunge until the ring is hit, and brought out. (This is Indian *poker*.)

---

1. In Passamaquoddy, *N'paowlin*: a man learned in mysteries, a scholar. This is my own Indian name. It is apparently the same with *boo-öin*, that is, pow-pow man. [CGL]

So, the evening passed, and nothing was said of marriage. At last, the guests went away, and for some time the young man made a jest of his having gone courting. One day he was far away and alone in the woods, when he met an old woman of very strange appearance. She was wrinkled and bent with extreme age, and her head was braided with a very great number of hair-strings, which hung down to her heels. After greeting him civilly, she asked him if he was really eager to marry one of the beauties whom he had visited. "Oh, grandmother," he replied, "I do not care about it."

"If you only did," she replied, "I could give you the one you want. You only need to say so."

Now the young man saw that the old woman was in earnest, and he replied that in fact he would be very glad to get one of the girls, but that no girl worth having would look at him. Then the old dame, taking one of her hair-strings, said, "Roll this up, and carry it in your pouch for a while,[2] and then go, and, when you have an opportunity, toss the cord upon her back. But take care that she does not know that you have done this, and let it be indeed a secret to all."

So, he took the hair-string and, visiting the girls once again, threw it on one of them, more hopeful of success this time. And the cast succeeded, though she said nothing then. But the next day, alone in the woods, he met her, for she had followed him. And she said, "Where are you going?"

"I am going hunting," he replied. "But, if you have not lost your way, what are you doing here?"

"I am not lost in the woods," she replied, but said no more.

Then, seeing how it was, he said, "It would be better, though, if I returned with you to your parents and told them that I found you lost and showed you the way home."

---

2. One of the infallible ancient methods to make anything into a fetish, or amulet, is to carry it a long time about the person. Familiarity, as Heine observes (*Reisebilder*), gives a silent life, or apparent sympathy, to even old clothes. Thus, domestic well-known objects become fairies, and thus they talk to children. [CGL]

After he did this, the girl's father perceived that she liked the young man and asked him if he wished to marry her. Since both were willing, and something more, the wedding feast was soon ready, the friends invited, and the couple settled down.

Some days after, the husband saw that his wife was wearing the magic hair-string and asked her, "Where did you get that pretty hair-string?"

"I found it," she replied, "in my usual sitting place in the wigwam." This caused the young man to reflect how kindly he had been treated by the old fairy or witch, and how easily he had won his wife without earning her and then to think of the deserving young chief's son who had failed. So, he took the chief's son into the woods where they found the old woman, who, kind as ever, did for the chief's son what she had already done for his friend and also gave him a magic hair-string. Soon thereafter, he used it in the same way and in like manner won the other sister. It was indeed good, for she was the one whom he wanted most. From then on, the two men whose wives were sisters, were on the best of terms and were often together.

Now the young chief reflected that his brother-in-law had been very kind to him for little cause, and he thought of some way he could repay him. So, he asked him one day if he would like to be a swift runner.

"Truly I would," replied the other.

"Then go and gather some feathers, and let them blow when the wind is high, and chase them. You will soon be able to outstrip the wind, and when the art comes, it will never depart from you."

Then he did this and became so swift that no man or beast could over-take him.

Once again, the chief's son said, "Would you like to become strong and very active?"

And as he, of course, said, "Yes," the friend replied, "Dress yourself in the worst and shabbiest garments, and attack the first man you encounter. He will catch you by the clothes, and you must slip out of them and run."

His friend did as he was told, and the first man whom he met was a lunatic, who gladly incited a fight. So, the young man slipped out of the clothes and ran, but the madman thought the apparel made the man, and so he beat it a long time and left it for dead. But the friend, who had escaped, did this with many men and indeed became strong and active.

Then the chief's son said, "I will teach you quickness of sight, so that you may perceive animals while hunting, though other men may not. Take a handful of moose's hairs and hold them firmly in a roll between your thumb and finger. Then hold them up in a high wind and let them go. Then you will be able to perceive, in time, all the moose. And to see deer, or any other animal, you must take their hair and treat it in the same way."

So, he did this and by means of this magic became so keen of sight that he beheld every beast. Yet again, the chief's son said, "Would you like to see birds where no other man can?"

And the young man consented and was told to strip the feathery part from a bird's quills, and, after blowing it into the air, he was to look carefully in the direction in which it flew. After practicing this for some time, he became very perfect in this art.[3]

Once he learned all these things, he asked the chief's son how he could learn to see the fish of the sea. In turn, he was told that he must collect all kinds of fish bones and burn them and pound them to dust. Consequently, he did this and, having blown them up into the wind, he could see all manner of fish and call them to him.

The young man contemplated deeply and reflected that the whales were giant-like in power. Therefore, he wondered what might be done through them by magic. And his friend said that it was true that the whales could give unearthly power to man and exceedingly long life. "Indeed," he said, "they never die until they are killed, and with their help, one may live on till life borders on immortality."

---

3. The secret of these spells is very apparent. But the teacher would make the pupil believe that the successful result would greatly depend on the color and kind of the fur or feathers employed. It is curious to observe how, in the over-refinement of sport among gentlemen, there is the idea that this or that is "good form" and "the correct thing." Whatever is done has to have the effect of establishing much which is a mere fetish: a fox in England and a bear in Canada must be killed in a certain way by men of caste. [CGL]

After hearing this, the young man burned a piece of whalebone and pounded it into powder. Then, standing on a rock that jutted out into the sea, the sorcerer blew the dust seawards. Before long, he saw dark spots far away, and as they grew to be more numerous, they became larger, and soon more numerous. With every grain of dust that he blew a whale came, and he blew again seven times. Then the whole school of immense creatures came towards him. The one that was largest, or the sagamore[4] of the whales, swam close to the man on the rock and said, "Why have you called me?"

And he replied, "Make me strong."

In turn, the Whale answered, "It is well. Put your hand in my mouth."

As he did this, he found and took out a golden key.

"Keep that," said the Whale. "While you have it, you will be safe against man, beast, or illness. The foe will not harm you; the spirits which haunt the wilderness will pass you by; hunger and pain will not know you; death will not be in your road."

So, the young man thanked the great magician and went home. Then, just as it had been promised, it came to pass. From then on, everything went well with him. Trouble and trial were with him no more. Those who were in his village never knew hunger. The wild game abounded and came to them when called. No enemy attacked them. The sun and moon smiled on them. They sang the songs of the olden time and played the flute in peace.

As time passed, the old chief drew near the end of his life, and his son asked the friend if his father's days could not be prolonged. But the magician thought it best to let him pass away in peace, and he did so. Then the young chief offered his place and power to his brother-in-law. But he refused it and spent his life in helping his friend in every way by his power and wisdom.

---

4. Chief.

The Chenoo, or The Story of a Cannibal with an Icy Heart

(Micmac and Passamaquoddy)

ONE AUTUMN AN INDIAN took his wife and their little boy and went far away to hunt in the northwest. After finding a fit place to pass the winter, they built a wigwam. The man brought home the game, the woman dressed and dried the meat, the small boy played about shooting birds with bow and arrow. In Indian-wise, all went well.

One afternoon, when the man was away and the wife, gathering wood, she heard a rustling in the bushes, as though some beast were brushing through them, and, as she looked up, she saw with horror something worse than the worst she had feared. It was an awful face glaring at her—something made of devil, man, and beast in their most dreadful forms. It was like a haggard old man with wolfish eyes. He was stark naked; his shoulders and lips were gnawed away, as if, when mad with hunger, he had eaten his own flesh. He carried a bundle on his back. The woman had heard of the terrible Chenoo, the creature who comes from the far, icy north, a creature, who is a man grown to be both devil and cannibal, and she saw at once that this was one of them.

Truly, she was in trouble, but dire need gives quick wit, as it was with this woman, who, instead of showing fear, ran up and addressed him with such fair words as "My dear father," pretending surprise and joy, and, telling him how glad her heart was, she asked where he had been so long. The Chenoo was amazed beyond measure at such a greeting where he expected yells and prayers, and in mute wonder let himself be led into the wigwam.

A wise and good woman, she took him inside and said she was sorry to see him so woebegone; she pitied his sad state; she brought a suit of her husband's clothes; she told him to dress himself and be cleaned. He did as she bade. He sat by the side of the wigwam and looked surly and sad, but kept quiet. It was all a new thing to him.

The woman arose and went out. She kept gathering sticks. The Chenoo rose and followed her. She was in great fear. "Now," she thought, "my death is near; now he will kill and devour me."

The Chenoo came to her and said, "Give me the axe!"

She gave it, and he began to cut down the trees. Man never saw such chopping! The great pines fell right and left, like summer saplings; the boughs were hewed and split as if by a tempest. She cried out, "My father, it's enough!"

He laid down the axe, walked into the wigwam, and sat down, always in grim silence. The woman gathered her wood and remained just as silent on the opposite side.

She heard her husband coming and ran out and told him everything. She asked him to do as she was doing. He thought it was a good idea. Then he went in and spoke kindly. He said, "My father-in-law," and asked where he had been so long. The Chenoo stared in amazement, but when he heard the man talk of all that had happened during the past years, his fierce face grew gentler.

They had their meal and offered him food, but he hardly touched it. He lay down to sleep. The man and his wife kept awake in terror. When the fire burned up, and it became warm, the Chenoo asked that a screen be placed before him. Since he was from the ice, he could not endure heat.

For three days he stayed in the wigwam; for three days he was sullen and grim. He hardly ate. Then he seemed to change. He spoke to the woman; he asked her if she had any tallow. She told him they had a good deal. He filled a large kettle; there was a gallon of it. He put it on the fire. When it was scalding hot, he drank it all off at a draught.

He became sick and grew pale. He cast up all the horrors and abominations of earth, things appalling to every sense. When it was all over, he seemed changed.[1] He lay down and slept. When he awoke, he asked for food and ate a good deal. From that time on, he was kind and good. They no longer feared him.

They lived on meat such as Indians prepare.[2] The Chenoo was tired of it. One day he said, "My daughter, don't you have any fresh meat?"

She said, "No."

When her husband returned, the Chenoo saw that there was black mud on his snowshoes. He asked him if there was a spring of water nearby. The friend said there was one that was half a day's journey distant.

"We must go there tomorrow," said the Chenoo.

And they went together, very early. The Indian was fleet in such running. But the old man, who seemed so wasted and worn, went on his snowshoes like the wind. They came to the spring. It was large and beautiful; the snow had all melted away around it; the border was flat and green.[3]

Then the Chenoo stripped himself and danced his magic dance around the spring. Soon the water began to foam and rise and fall, as if some monster below were heaving in accord with the steps and the song. The Chenoo danced faster and wilder; then the head of an immense *Taktalok*, or lizard, rose above the surface. The old man killed it with a blow of his hatchet. Dragging it out, he began again to dance. He brought out another, the female, not so large, but still heavy as an elk. They were small spring lizards, but the Chenoo had conjured them, and by his magic they were turned into monsters.

---

1. The Chenoo is not only a cannibal, but a ghoul. He preys on nameless horrors. In this case, "having yielded to the power of kindness, he has made up his mind to partake of the food and hospitality of his hosts. To change his life; but to adapt his system to the new regimen he must thoroughly clear it of the old."—*Rand manuscript*. This is a very naïve and curious Indian conception of moral reformation. It appears to be a very ancient eskimo tale, recast in modern time by some zealous recent Christian convert. [CGL]

2. That is, cured, dried, smoked meat and then packed and pressed in large blocks. [CGL]

3. Not uncommon around warm springs even in midwinter, and among ice and snow. [CGL]

He dressed the game; he cut it up. He took the heads and feet and tails and all that he did not want, and threw them back into the spring. "They will grow again into many lizards," he said.

When the meat was trimmed, it looked like that of the bear. He bound it together with withes; he took it on his shoulders; he ran like the wind; his load was nothing. The Indian was a great runner; nobody in the entire land could compare to him, but now he lagged far behind.

"Can you go no faster than that?" asked the Chenoo. "The sun is setting; the red will soon be black. At this rate, it will be dark ere we get home. Get on my shoulders."

The Indian mounted on the load. The Chenoo told him to hold his head low, so that he would not be knocked off by the branches. "Brace your feet," he said, "so you can be steady."

Then the old man flew like the wind; the bushes whistled as they flew past them. They got home before sunset.

The wife was afraid to touch such meat.[4] But her husband was persuaded to eat some. It was like bear's meat. The Chenoo fed on it. So, they all lived as friends.

Then spring arrived. One day, the Chenoo told them that something terrible would soon happen. An enemy, a Chenoo, a woman, was coming like wind, yes—on the wind—from the north to kill him. There could be no escape from the battle. She would be far more furious, mad, and cruel than any male, even one of his own cruel race, could be. He did not know how the battle would end, but the man and his wife had to be put in a place of safety. To keep from hearing the terrible war-whoops of the Chenoo, which is death to mortals, their ears had to be closed. They had to hide themselves in a cave.

Then he sent the woman for the bundle which he had brought with him, and which had hung untouched on a branch of a tree since he had been with them. Before she left, he said, if she found anything in it offensive to her to throw it away, but to certainly bring him a smaller bundle which was inside the other. So, she went and opened it, and there were a pair of human

---

4. "The Indians are much less particular than white men as to food, but they avoid *choojeeck*, or reptiles."—*Rand manuscript*. [CGL]

legs and feet inside as well as the remains of some earlier horrid meal. She threw them far away. The small bundle she brought to him.

The Chenoo opened it and took out a pair of horns—horns of the dragon. One of them had two branches; the other was straight and smooth. They were golden-bright. He gave the straight horn to the Indian and kept the other. He said that these were magical weapons, and the only ones of any use for the coming fight. So, they waited for the foe.

And the third day came. The Chenoo was fierce and bold; he listened; he had no fear. He heard the long and awful scream—like nothing on earth—of the enemy, as she sped through the air far away in the icy north, long before the others could hear it. And everything would be like this: if they were to live without harm after hearing the first deadly yell of the enemy, they would not suffer harm, and if they heard the answering shout of their friend, all would be well with them.[5] But he said, "Should you hear me call for help, then hasten with the horn, and you may save my life."

They did as he requested. They stuffed their ears; they hid in a deep hole dug in the ground. Then, all at once, the cry of the foe burst on them like screaming thunder; their ears rang with pain: they were almost killed, despite all the care they had taken. But then they heard the answering cry of their friend and were no longer in danger from mere noise.

The battle began, the fight was fearful. The monsters, enraged by their magic, rose to the size of mountains. The tall pines were torn up; the ground trembled as in an earthquake; rocks crashed upon rocks; the conflict deepened and darkened; no tempest was ever so terrible. Then the male Chenoo was heard crying: "My son-in-law, come and help me!"

He ran to the fight. What he saw was terrible! The Chenoos, who, if they had stood upright, would have risen far above the clouds as giants of hideous form, were struggling on the ground. The female seemed to be the conqueror. She was holding her foe down. She knelt on him and was doing all she could to thrust her dragon's horn into his ear. And he, to avoid death,

---

5. In all this, we clearly perceive the horrible scream of the *angakok*, or Eskimo Shaman, trained through years and generations to utter sounds which terrify even brave men. [CGL]

was moving his head rapidly from side to side, while she, mocking his cries, said, "You have no son-in-law to help you. I'll take your cursed life and eat your liver."

The Indian was so small alongside these giants that the female Chenoo did not notice him.

"Now," said his friend, "thrust the horn into her ear!"

He did this with a well-directed blow and struck hard. The point entered her head. As it touched, it sprouted quick as a flash of lightning and darted through the head. It came out of the other ear and had become like a long pole. As it touched the ground, it struck downward and took deep and firm root.

The male Chenoo told him to raise the other end of the horn and place it against a large tree. He did so. It coiled itself around the tree like a snake and grew rapidly. The enemy was held hard and fast. Then the two began to dispatch her. It was long and weary work. To be killed at all, such a being must be hewed into small pieces; flesh and bones must all be utterly consumed by fire. Should the least fragment remain unburnt, a grown Chenoo would spring from it with all the force and fire of the first.[6]

Once the fury of battle was past, the Chenoos returned to their usual size. The victor hewed the enemy to small pieces, to be revenged for the insult and threat with regard to eating his liver. Having roasted that part of his captive, he ate it before her while she was still alive. He told her she was served as she would have served him.

But the hardest task of all was to come. It was to burn or melt the heart. It was of ice, and more than ice—it is much colder, as ice is colder than fire, much harder as ice is harder than water. When placed in the fire, it put out the flame. Yet, by long burning, it melted slowly, until they at last broke it into fragments with a hatchet, and then melted these. Then they returned to the camp.

---

6. The idea is common to both Eskimo and Indian that so long as a fragment of a body remains unburned, the being, man or beast, may, by magic, be revived from it. It was probably suggested by observing the great vitality and power of self-production inherent in many lower forms of life, and may have given rise to the belief in vampires. [CGL]

Spring came. The snows of winter, as water, ran down the rivers to the sea. The ice and snow, which had encamped on the inland hills, sought the shore. So did the Indian and his wife. The Chenoo, with softened soul, went with them. Now he was becoming a man like other men. Before going, they built a canoe for the old man. They did not cover it with birch bark; they made it of moose-skin. In it they placed a part of their venison and skins. The Chenoo took his place in the canoe. They took the lead, and he followed.

And, after winding on with the river, down rapids and under forest-boughs, they came out into the sunshine, on a broad, beautiful lake. But suddenly, when midway in the water, the Chenoo laid flat in the canoe, as if to hide himself. Immediately, he explained that he had just then been discovered by another Chenoo, who was standing on the top of a mountain, whose dim blue outline could just be seen stretching far away to the north.

"He has seen me," he said, "but he cannot see you. Nor can he behold me now, but should he discover me again, his wrath will be roused. Then he will attack me. I don't know who might conquer. I prefer peace."

So, he lay hidden, and they took his canoe in tow. But when they had crossed the lake and come to the river again, the Chenoo said that he could not travel further by water. He would walk through the woods, but he would no longer sail on streams. Then they told him where they meant to camp that night. He started over mountains and through woods and up rocks, a far, round-about journey. And the man and his wife went down the river in a spring freshet, headlong with the rapids. But when they had paddled round the point where they meant to pass the night, they saw smoke rising among the trees, and on landing they found the Chenoo sleeping soundly by the fire which had been built for them.

This he repeated for several days. But as they went south, a great change came over him. He was a being of the north. Ice and snow had no effect on him, but he could not endure the soft airs of summer. He grew weaker and weaker. When they had reached their village, he had to be carried like a little child. He had grown gentle. His fierce and formidable face was now like that of a man. His wounds had healed; his teeth no longer grinned wildly all the time. The people gathered round him in wonder.

He was dying. This was after the white men had come. They sent for a priest, who found the Chenoo as ignorant of all religion as a wild beast. At first, he would repel the father in anger. Then he listened and learned the truth. As a result, the old heathen's heart changed; he was deeply moved. He asked to be baptized, and as the first tear which he had ever shed in all his life came to his eyes, he died.

The Giant Magicians

(Micmac)

THERE WAS ONCE A man and his wife who lived by the sea far away from other people. They had many children, and they were very poor. One day this couple was in a canoe far from land. A dense fog arose, and they became quite lost. As they drifted, they heard a noise sounding like paddles and voices. The noise drew nearer. Then they dimly saw a monstrous canoe filled with giants, who greeted the little folk like friends.

"My little brother," said the leader, "where are you going?"

"I am lost in the fog," the poor Indian replied very sadly.

"Ah, come with us to our camp," said the giant, who seemed to be a good fellow, if there ever was one. "Truly, you will be well treated, my small friends, for my father is the chief. So, be of good cheer!"

Since the man and his wife were very amazed by this gentleness, they sat still in awe, while two of the giants put the tips of their paddles under their bark, lifted it up, and put it into their own, as if it had been a chip. And truly, the giants seemed to be as much pleased with the little folk as a boy would be who had found a flying squirrel.[1] As they drew near the beach, the couple beheld three wigwams, high as mountains to match the size of the giants. Soon the chief, who was taller than the rest, came to meet them.

"Ha!" he cried. "Son, what have you there? Where did you pick up that little brother?"

---

1. A story like this of giants in a canoe would very naturally originate in the vicinity of the Bay of Fundy, where in the dense and frequent fogs, all objects assume greatly exaggerated apparent dimensions. One often beholds there, on the shore, "men as trees walking." [CGL]

"I found him lost in the fog, my father."

"Well, bring him home to the lodge, my son."

So, the giant took the small canoe in the palm of his hand. The man and his wife were sitting in it, and yet, he carried them home. Then they were taken into the wigwam, and the canoe was laid carefully in the eaves, but within easy reach, about a hundred and fifty yards from the ground.

Then an abundant meal was set before them, but the benevolent host, mindful of their small size, did not give them more to eat than they would have needed for about ten years to come, and informed them in a subdued whisper, which could have been heard a hundred miles away, that his name was Oscoon.[2]

Now it came to pass a few days after that a company of these well-grown people went hunting, and when they returned, the guests had to pity them because they had no game in their land appropriate for their size. Indeed, they returned from their hunt with strings of such small affairs as two or three dozen caribou hanging in their belts, as a Micmac might carry a string of squirrels, and they also swung one or two moose in their bands like rabbits. Yet, with these and many deer, bears, and beavers that made up in the weight of their game, they were generous with all they brought, no matter the size.

Now the giants became very fond of the small folk, and they would do anything in the world to make sure that they would never be harmed. Then, one morning, the chief came and told them that there would soon be a great battle because they expected to be attacked by a Chenoo in three days. Therefore, the Micmac saw that, just as their people had troubles in all things with the wicked at their home, the giants also had the same problems. The chiefs were obliged to do their share and to keep up their magic and know all that was going on in the world. In fact, he would be a poor *powwow* and a necromancer worth nothing if he could not foretell such a trifle as the day and hour when an enemy would be on them.

But this time the Sagamore was forewarned and told his little guests to stuff their ears and bind up their heads, and roll themselves in many folds of dressed skins, otherwise, they would hear the deadly war-scream of the Chenoo.

---

2. The dark color of his tribe. Eskimo legends speak of people among them who were black. [CGL]

They did as they were told. Nevertheless, despite all their care, they hardly survived the battle cries. Then, the second scream hurt them less, and after the third, the chief came to them with a cheerful countenance and told them to arise and unpack themselves, for the monster was slain, and though his four sons, with two other giants, had been sorely tried, they had conquered the Chenoo.

However, the sorrows of the good are never at an end, and so it was with these honest giants, who were always being pestered by some kind of scurvy knaves or others who would not leave them in peace. Soon, the chief announced that this time a Kookwes—a burly, beastly villain, not much better than his cousin the Chenoo—was coming to play at rough murder with them. Verily, by this time the Micmac began to believe, without betting an ace on it, that all of these tall people were like the wolves, who, meeting with nobody else, bite one another. So, the small folk were bound and bundled up as before and put to bed like dolls. And again they heard the horrible shout, the moderate shout, and the smaller shout, until *sooel moonoodooahdigool*, which means that they hardly heard him at all.

Then, the warriors returned and gave proof that they had indeed done something more than kick the wind. Indeed, they were covered with blood, and their legs were stuck full of large pines and here and there an oak or hemlock because the fight had been in a forest so that they had been as much troubled as men would be with thistles, nettles, and pine splinters, which is truly often a great trouble. But this was their least problem. As they told their chief, the enemy had well-nigh made Jack Drum's entertainment for them and would have led them to the devil's dance, had not one of them, by good luck, opened his eyes for him with a rock which drove it into his brain. And as it was, the chief's youngest son had been so mauled that, coming home, he fell dead right in front of his father's door. Truly, this might have been deemed almost an accident in some families. But look! What a good thing it is to have an enchanter in the house, especially one who knows his business, as did the old chief, who, going out, asked the young man why he was lying there. To which he replied that it was because he was dead. Then his father told to him to stand and walk, which he did and went straight to the supper table and ate none the less for it.

Now, thinking that perhaps his dear little people found life dull and devoid of incident with him, the old chief asked them if they were weary of him. In turn, they answered with golden truth that they had never been so merry, but they were anxious about their children at home. He answered that they were indeed right, and that the next morning they could depart. So, the next day, the giants fetched their canoe for them and packed it full of the finest furs and best meat. Then, they were told to get in and were followed by a small dog, solemnly charged to take the people home, while the people were told to paddle in the direction in which the dog pointed.[3] Finally, the chief said to the Micmac, "Seven years from now, you will be reminded of me." And then, off they went!

The man took a seat in the stern, his wife in the prow, and the dog sat in the middle of the canoe. The dog pointed, the Indian paddled, the water was smooth. They soon reached home, and their children ran to meet them with joy, while the dog cheerfully ran to see the children, wagging his tail with great glee, just as if he had been like any other dog, and not a fairy. Once he made their acquaintance, he soon turned tail and trotted off for home again, running over the ocean surface as if it had been hard ice. This incident might, indeed, have once astonished the good man and his wife, but they had lately seen so many wonders that they were past marveling.

Now, this Indian, who had in the past always been poor, seemed to have quite recovered from that dilemma. When he let down his lines, the biggest fish bit, and all his sprats were salmon. He prayed for goslings and got geese. Moose were just like mice to him now. He even had the best and fattest in the land. So, seven years passed, and then, as he slept, he had diverse dreams, and in them he went back to the Land of the Giants and saw all those who had been so kind to him. And another night, he dreamed again that he was standing by his wigwam near the sea, and that a great whale swam up to him and began to sing. Indeed, the singing was the sweetest he had ever heard.

Then he remembered that the giant had told him he would think of him in seven years, and now he clearly understood what it all meant—that he

---

3. Strange as it may seem, there is not the least exaggeration in this. Lieutenant-Colonel Barclay Kennan told me that when surveying in the far North Pacific he had an Eskimo dog, which, in the thickest fog, would scent the land at a great distance, and continually point to it. [CGL]

was soon to have magical power given to him, and that he would become a *Megumoowessoo*. After he told his wife, who was not learned in mysterious lore, she was glad to know more about what kind of a being he expected to be, and whether a spirit or a man, good or bad. All this was, indeed, not easy to explain, nor is it clearly set down in the chronicles beyond this—that, whatever it might be, it was all for the best, and that there was a great deal of magic in it.

That day they saw a great shark cruising about in their bay, chasing fish, and they took this for an evil omen. But, soon after, the same small dog, who had been their pilot from the Land of the Giants, came trotting towards them over the sea. Just as before, he was full of joy at seeing them and the children, and wagged his tail and danced for glee. Then, he looked earnestly at the man as if for some message. In turn, the man said to him, "It is well. In three years' time I will visit you, and I will look to the southwest."

Then the dog licked the hands and the ears and the eyes of the man, and went home as before, running over the sea on the water.

And when the three years had passed, the Indian got into his canoe, and, paddling without fear, found his way to the Land of the Giants. He saw the wigwams standing on the beach. The immense canoes were drawn up on the water's edge. From afar he beheld the old giant coming down to welcome him, but he was alone. Later, after the Indian had been welcomed and was in the wigwam, he learned that all the sons were dead. They had died three years ago, when the shark, the great sorcerer, had been seen.

They had passed away, and the old man had but lingered a little longer. They had made the magic change. They had departed, and he would soon join them in his own kingdom. But before he went, he wanted to leave their great inheritance, their magic, to the man.

After telling him all this, the giant brought out one of his son's clothes and told the Indian to put them on. Truly, this was as if he had been asked to clothe himself with a great house because the smallest fold was like a cavern. But he stepped in, and as he did this, he rose to a great size. He filled out the garments until they fit. He was now a giant of Giant-Land. With the clothes came the wisdom, the *m'teoulin*, the *manitou* power of the greatest and wisest of the olden days. He was indeed *Megumoowessoo* and had attained the Mystery.

The Girl–Chenoo

(Micmac)

FAR UP THE SAGUENAY River a branch turns off to the north, running back into the land of ice and snow. Ten families went up this stream one autumn in their canoes to be gone all winter on a hunt. Among them was a beautiful girl, twenty years of age. A young man in the band wished her to become his wife, but she flatly refused him. Perhaps she did it in such a way as to wound his pride. Certainly, she roused all that was savage in him, and he could think of nothing else but revenge.

Since he was skilled in medicine and magic, he went into the woods and gathered an herb, which makes people insensible. Then stealing into the lodge when all were asleep, he held it to the girl's face until she had inhaled the odor and could not be easily awakened. As he left, he made a ball of snow, and after returning, he placed it in the hollow of her neck, in front, just below the throat. Then he retired without being discovered. As long as the chill went to her heart, she could not wake up.[1]

When she awoke, she was chilly, shivering, and sick. She refused to eat. This lasted a long time, and her parents became alarmed. They asked her what was troubling her. She was ill-tempered and said that nothing was the matter. One day, having been sent to the spring for water, she remained

---

1. The Eskimo Shamans and the Indian *boo-oin* are familiar with many very ingenious and singular ways of producing prolonged illness and death. There is one known to a very few old gypsies of gradually inducing insanity and death, which I have never seen noted in any work on toxicology. In a work which I recently read, the author denied there was any such thing as a "lingering poison"! [CGL]

absent so long that her mother went to look for her. Approaching unseen, she observed her daughter greedily eating snow. After she asked her what this meant, the daughter explained that she felt a burning sensation inside her that the snow relieved. More than that, she craved the snow; the taste of it was pleasant to her.

After a few days, she began to grow fierce, as though she wished to kill someone. At last, she begged her parents to kill her. Until then, she had loved them very much. Now she told them that unless they killed her, she would certainly be their death. Her whole nature was in the process of being changed.

"How can we kill you?" her mother asked.

"You must shoot me," she replied, "with seven arrows.[2] And if you can kill me with seven shots, all will be well. But if you cannot, I shall kill you."

Seven men shot at her, as she sat in the wigwam. She was not bound. Every arrow struck her in the breast, but she sat firm and unmoved. Forty-nine times they pierced her, and from time to time, she looked up with an encouraging smile. When the last arrow struck, she fell dead.

Then they burned the body, as she had instructed them to do. It was soon reduced to ashes with the exception of the heart, which was of the hardest ice. This required much time to melt and break. At last, all was over.

She had been brought under the power of an evil spirit and was rapidly being changed into a Chenoo, a wild, fierce, unconquerable being. But she knew it all the time, and it was against her will. That is why she had begged them to kill her.

The Indians left the place, and ever since that day, none have ever returned to it. They were afraid that some small part of her body might have remained unconsumed, and another Chenoo might rise, capable of killing all whom she met.

---

2. The Micmac version gives *guns*. But the Chenoo stories are evidently very ancient and refer to terrors of the olden time.

The Invisible One

(Micmac)

THERE WAS ONCE A large Indian village situated on the border of a lake. At the end of the place was a lodge, in which a strange creature dwelt, and he was always invisible. He had a sister who attended to his wants, and it was known that any girl who managed to see him would be chosen to marry him. Therefore, there were few, indeed, who did not try, but it was long before one succeeded. And this is how it happened.

Towards evening, when the Invisible One was supposed to be returning home, his sister would walk with any of the girls who came down to the shore of the lake. She, in fact, could see her brother, since he was always visible to her. Whenever she perceived him, she would ask her companions, "Do you see my brother?"

And then they would mostly answer, "Yes," though some said, "Nay." And then the sister would ask, "What is the material of his shoulder-strap?"

But as some tell the tale, she would inquire about other things such as: "What is his moose-runner's haul?" "What does he use to draw his sled?"

And they would reply, "a strip of rawhide," or "a green withe," or something of the kind. And then she would know they had not told the truth and would reply quietly, "Very well, let us return to the wigwam!"

And when they entered the place, she would tell them not to take a certain seat, for it was his. And after they had helped to cook the supper, they would wait with great curiosity to see him eat. Truly, he gave proof that he was a real person, for as he took off his moccasins, they became visible, and his sister hung them up. But beyond this, they saw nothing, not even when they remained all night, as many did.

Now, an old man, a widower, with three daughters, dwelt in the village. The youngest of these was very small, weak, and often ill, which did not prevent her sisters, especially the eldest, treating her with great cruelty. The second daughter was kinder and sometimes took the side of the poor abused girl, but the other would burn her hands and face with hot coals. Yes, her whole body was scarred with the marks made by torture, so that people called her the rough-faced girl. And whenever her father came home and asked why the child was so disfigured, her sisters would promptly say that it was the fault of the girl herself. She had been forbidden to go near the fire, and when she had disobeyed, she had fallen in.

Now it occurred to the two elder sisters of this poor girl to go and try their luck at seeing the Invisible One. So, they dressed themselves in their finest and tried to look their fairest. After finding his sister at home, they went with her to take the designated walk down to the water. Then, when the Invisible One came, they were asked if they saw him.

"Certainly," they said and replied to the questions about the shoulder-strap or sled cord, "A piece of rawhide." In doing so, they revealed they had lied, like the rest, for they had seen nothing and received nothing for their pains.

When their father returned home the next evening, he brought with him many of the pretty little shells from which wampum was made,[1] and they were soon engaged in stringing them.

That day poor little Oochigeaskw, the burnt-faced girl, who had always run barefoot, got a pair of her father's old moccasins and put them into water so that they might become flexible to wear. Then she begged her sisters for a few wampum shells, and the eldest just called her "a lying little pest," but the other gave her a few. Since Oochigeaskw had no clothes beyond a few paltry rags, the poor creature went forth and fetched a few sheets of birch bark from the woods. Then she made a dress out of the birch bark and put some figures on it. Finally, she shaped this dress like those worn of old. Afterward, she made a petticoat and a loose gown, a cap, leggings, and

---

1. In Passamaquoddy, wampum is called *waw-bap*. It is said that a single bead required a full day's work to make and finish it. [CGL]

handkerchief. Then, she put on her father's great old moccasins, which came nearly up to her knees, and she went forth to try her luck. For even this little thing wanted to see the Invisible One in the great wigwam at the end of the village.

Truly, she had a most inauspicious beginning, for there was one long storm of ridicule and hisses, yells and hoots, from her own door to that which she went to seek. Her sisters tried to shame her and told her to stay at home, but she would not obey, and all the idlers, upon seeing this strange little creature in her odd array, cried, "Shame!" But she kept walking, for she was greatly determined. Indeed, it may be that some spirit had inspired her.

Now this poor small wretch in her self-made attire, with her hair singed off and her little face as full of burns and scars as there are holes in a sieve, was, for all this, most kindly received by the sister of the Invisible One. Indeed, this noble girl knew more than the mere outside of things as the world knows them. And as the brown of the evening sky became black, she took her down to the lake. Before long, the girls sensed that he had come. Then the sister said, "Do you see him?"

And the other replied with awe, "Truly I do,—and he is wonderful."

"And what is his sled-string?"

"It is," she replied with fear, "the rainbow."

"Now, my sister," said the other, "what is his bow-string?"

"His bowstring is the Spirits' Road, the Milky Way."[2]

"You have *seen* him," the sister said and took the girl home and bathed her. As she washed her, all the scars disappeared from her face and body. Her hair grew again; it was very long and like a blackbird's wing. Her eyes were like stars. Nobody in the entire world was as beautiful as she was. Then, the sister of the Invincible One went to her treasures, gave her a wedding

---

2. The Spirits' or Ghosts' Road, so called because it is believed to be the highway by which spirits pass to and from the earth. The Micmac version, belittled and reduced in every way, limits this reply to "a piece of rainbow." There is a grandeur of conception in the Passamaquoddy myth, which recalls the most stupendous similes in Scripture. [CGL]

garment and adorned her. As she combed her, her hair grew. It was a great marvel to behold.

Then, after doing this, she told her to take the *wife's seat* in the wigwam. It was next to her brother's seat at the door. And when he entered, terrible and beautiful, he smiled and said, "So I have been seen!"

"Yes," Oochigeaskw replied and thus became his wife.

The Young Man Who Was Saved by a Rabbit and a Fox

(Passamaquoddy)

A MAN AND HIS wife dwelled in the woods far away from other people.[1] They had one boy, who grew up strong and clever. One day he said, "Father and mother, let me go and see other men and women."

They grieved, but let him go. He went far away. All night he lay on the ground. In the morning he heard something coming. He rose and saw it was a Rabbit, who said, "Ha, friend, where are you going?"

The boy answered, "To find people."

"That is what I want," replied the Rabbit. "Let us go together."

So they went on for a long time until they heard voices far off and walked quietly to a village.

"Now," said the Rabbit to the boy, "sneak unseen and listen to them!"

The boy did so and heard the people saying that a kewahqu, or cannibal monster, was to come the next day to devour the daughter of the Sagamore.

---

1. This story, narrated by Tomah Josephs, is partly old Indian and partly European, but whether the latter element was derived from a French Canadian or a Norse source I cannot tell, since it is common to both. The mention of the horse and the hog, or of cattle, does not prove that a story is not pre-Columbian. The Norsemen had brought cattle of various descriptions even to New England. It is to be very much regretted that the first settlers in New England took no pains to ascertain what the Indians knew of the white men who had preceded them. But modern material may have easily been added to an old legend. [CGL]

After returning and reporting this to the Rabbit, the latter said to the boy, "Have no fear. Go to the people and tell them that you can save her."

He did so, but it took a long time before they would listen to him. Yet, at last, the old chief heard that a strange young man insisted that he could save the girl. So, the chief sent for him and said, "They tell me that you think you can deliver my daughter from death. Do so, and she will be yours."

Then the young man returned to the Rabbit, who said, "They did not send the girl far away because they know that the demon can follow any track. But I hope to make a track which he cannot follow. Now, as soon as it is dark, I want you to bring her to this place."

The young man did so, and the Rabbit was there with a sled, and in his hand he had two squirrels. These he smoothed down, and as he did so, they grew to be as large as the largest sled-dogs. Then all three went headlong, like the wind, until they came to another village.

The Rabbit looked about, and once he found a certain wigwam, he peered through a crevice into the wigwam.

"This is the place," he said. "Enter."

They did so. Then the Rabbit ran away. They found an old woman, who was very kind, but who, on seeing them, burst into tears.

"Ah, my dear grandchildren," she cried, "your death is following you rapidly, for the kewahqu is on your track and will soon be here. So, be quick and run down to the river, where you will find your grandfather camping."

They went and were joined by the Rabbit, who had spent some time in making many divergent tracks in the ground. Soon the kewahqu came. The tracks delayed him a long time, but at last, he found the right one. Meanwhile the young couple went on and found an old man by the river. "Truly," he said, "you are in great danger, for the kewahqu is coming. But I will help you." Upon saying this, he threw himself into the water, where he floated with outstretched limbs and said, "Now, my children, get on me."

The girl was afraid of falling off the old man, but after being reassured, she mounted, and he turned into a canoe, which carried them safely across. But when they turned to look at him, lo and behold! He was no longer a canoe, but an old duck.

"Now, my dear children," he said, "rush to the top of the mountain over there, high among the gray rocks. There you will find your friend."

They fled to the old gray mountain. The kewahqu came raging and roaring in a fury, but no matter how he pursued, they arrived at the foot of the precipice before him. There stood the Rabbit. He was holding up a very long pole. No pine was ever longer.

"Climb this," he said.

As they climbed, it became even longer. Then they left it for the hill and scrambled up the rocks. Soon the kewahqu came yelling and howling horribly. Seeing the fugitives far above, he swarmed up the pole. With him, too, it grew, and grew rapidly, until it seemed to be half a mile high. Now the kewahqu was not the kind of sorcerer who could fly. Since he did not have wings, he had to remain on the pole. Then, when he came to the top, the young man pushed it away. The pole fell, and the monster was killed by the fall.

Now they rode away on the squirrel-sled. They flew through the woods over the snow by the moonlight. They were very glad. When they finally arrived at the girl's village, the Rabbit said, "My, friends, good-bye. There is more trouble coming, and when it comes upon you, I and mine will help you. So farewell."

Finally, they reached home again, and it all appeared like a dream. Then the wedding feast was held, and all seemed well. But the young men of the village hated the outsider and desired to kill him so that they might take his wife. They persuaded him to go fishing with them on the sea. Then they uttered a cry and yelled, "A whale is chasing us. He's under the canoe!"

Then, suddenly they knocked him overboard and paddled away like an arrow soaring in the air. The young man called for help. A crow came and said, "Swim or float as long as you can. I will bring you help."

He floated a long time. The crow returned with a strong cord and made himself very large. He threw one end of the cord to the young man and towed him to a small island with the other end.

"I can do no more," he said, "but there is another friend."

So, as the young man sat there, starving and freezing, a fox came to him.

"Ha, friend," he said, "are you here?"

"Yes," replied the youth, "and I'm dying of hunger."

The fox reflected an instant and said, "Truly, I have no meat, but there is a way."

So, he picked a blade of dry grass from the ground and told the young man to eat it. He did so and found himself transformed into a moose. Then he fed richly on the young grass until he had enough. When the fox gave him a second straw, he became a man again.

"Friend," said the fox, "there is an Indian village on the mainland, where there is to be a great feast, a grand dance. Would you like to go there?"

"Indeed, I would," replied the young man. "Then wait till dark, and I will take you there," said the fox.

And when night came, he told the young man to close his eyes and enter the river and take hold of the end of his tail, while he would pull him. So, they went on for hours in the turbulent sea.

The young man thought, "We shall never get there."

But the fox said, "Yes, we will, but keep your eyes shut."

So, it went on for another hour, when the young man remarked again, "We shall never reach land."

And again the fox said, "Yes, we shall."

Indeed, after some time passed, the young man opened his eyes. They were only ten feet from the shore, and this cost them more time and trouble than all the previous swimming before they had the beach under their feet.

It was his own village. The festival was for the marriage of his own wife to one of the young men who had pushed him overboard. Great was his magic power, great was his anger. He became as strong as death. Then he went to his own wigwam. His wife cried aloud for joy upon seeing him. She kissed him and wept all at once.

"Be glad," he said, "but the hour of punishment for the men who made these tears has come."

So, he went to the Sagamore and told him everything. In turn, the old chief called for the young men.

"Slay them all as you choose," he said to his son-in-law. "Scalp them."

But the young man refused. He called to the fox and got the straws which gave him the power to transform men into beasts. Then he changed his enemies into nasty animals—one into a porcupine, one into a hog—and they were driven into the woods. Thus, it was that the first hog and the first porcupine came into the world.

The Mournful Mystery of the Partridge–Witch, or How a Young Man Died from Love

(Passamaquoddy)

TWO BROTHERS WENT HUNTING during autumn and got as far as the headwaters of the Penobscot, where they remained all winter.[1] But in March their snowshoes gave out, as did their moccasins, and they wished that a woman were there to mend them.

When the younger brother returned first to the lodge, the next day—which he generally did, to get it ready for the elder—he was astonished to find that someone had been there before him and had done the housekeeping. Indeed, garments had been mended, the place cleaned and swept, a fire built, and the pot was boiling. He said nothing of this to his brother, but when he returned the next day at the same time, he found that all had been attended to just as before. And again he said nothing, but in the morning, when he went forth to hunt, he went only a little way. Then he returned, found a place to hide, and watched the door to the lodge. All at once, a beautiful and graceful girl, well attired, arrived and entered the wigwam. Then he stepped softly, looked through a hole in the lodge, and saw her very busy with his housekeeping.

---

1. This tale is reminiscent of the famous story of *Undine* and was told to Leland by Tomah Josephs, a Passamaquoddy Indian. [CGL]

When he entered, she seemed to be greatly alarmed and confused, but he calmed her, and they soon became good friends, playing together very happily all day long like children, for indeed they were both young. When the sun's height was low and his shadows long, the girl said, "I must go now. I hear your brother coming, and I fear him. But I will return tomorrow. *Addio!*"

So, she went, and the elder brother knew nothing of what had happened. The next day she came again, and once more they played in sunshine and shadow until evening. However, before she went, he sought to persuade her to remain forever. And she reacted in doubt and answered, "Tell your brother everything, and it may be that I will stay and serve you both. I can make the snowshoes and moccasins which you need so much, and also canoes."

Then she departed with the day, and the elder brother returned and listened to everything that had happened from his brother.

"Truly," he said, "I would be glad to have someone here to take care of the wigwam and make snowshoes."

Consequently, she came in the morning, and when she heard from the young man that his brother had consented to her coming, she was very glad and hastily went away. But she returned about noon, drawing a toboggan piled up with garments and arms, for she was a huntress. Indeed, she could do things few women could do, whether it was cooking, needlework, or making things that all men need. And the winter passed very pleasantly until the snow grew soft, and it was time for them to return. Up to the time she had arrived, they had had little luck in hunting, but after her arrival, everything had gone well with them, and they now had a wonderful quantity of furs.

Then they returned to their village in a canoe, going down the river. But as they approached, the girl grew sad, for she had thrown out her soul to their home by *meelahbi-give*,[2] though they were not aware of it. And suddenly she said, as they came to a point of land, "I must leave you here. I can go no further. Say nothing of me to your parents, for your father would have but little love for me."

---

2. Passamaquoddy: Clairvoyance, or state of vision. [CGL]

And the young men sought to persuade her, but she only answered sorrowfully, "It cannot be."

So they went home with their furs, and the elder was so proud of their luck and their strange adventure that he could not hold his peace, but told everything. Then his father was very angry and said, "All my life have I feared this. Know that this woman was a devil of the woods, a witch, and a sister of the goblins and ghosts."

And he spoke so earnestly and so long of this thing that they were afraid, and the elder brother was so persuaded by his father that he went forth to slay her, and the younger followed him from afar. They soon found her bathing in the stream, and when she saw them, she ran up a little hill. As she ran, the elder shot an arrow at her. All at once, there was a strange flurry about her, a fluttering of scattered feathers, and the brothers saw her fly away as a partridge. When they returned to their wigwam, they told their father what had happened, and he said, "You did well. I know all about these female devils who seek to destroy men. Verily this was a she-Wikumwess."[3]

But the younger brother could not forget her and longed to see her again. So, one day he went into the woods, and there he indeed found her, and she was as kind as before. Then he said, "Truly it was not by my good will that my brother shot at you."

And she answered, "I know that very well, and that your father caused this. Yet, I don't blame him, for this is an affair from the days of old; and even yet, it is not at an end, and the greatest is to come. But let the day be only a day unto itself; the things of tomorrow are for tomorrow, and those of yesterday are departed."

So, they forgot their troubles and played together merrily all day long in the woods and in the open places, and told stories of old times till sunset. And as the crow went to his tree, the boy said, "I must return."

And she replied, "Whenever you want to see me, come to the woods. And remember what I say. Do not marry anyone else. For your father wishes

---

3. The Wikumwess is a Robin Goodfellow, who plays pranks on people, or treats them kindly, according to his caprice. [CGL]

you to do so, and he will speak of it to you, and he'll do that soon. Yet, it is for your sake only that I say this."

Then she told him word by word everything that his father had said, but he was not astonished, for now he knew that she was not like other women, but he did not care about this. And he grew brave and bold, and then he was above all things. And when she told him that if he should marry another, he would surely die, it did not mean anything to him.

Then, as soon as he returned to the village, the first thing his father said was, "My son, I have provided a wife for you, and the wedding must be at once."

And he said, "It is well. Let it be so."

Then the bride came. For four days they held the wedding dance; four days they feasted. But, on the last day, he said, "This is the end of it all," and he laid himself down on a white bearskin, and a great sickness came upon him. By the time they brought the bride to him he was dead.

Truly the father knew what ailed him, and even more, but he said nothing. Now, since the place no longer pleased him, he and his family departed and scattered far and wide.

The Three Strong Men

(Micmac)

THERE WAS A CHIEFTAIN in the days of yore.[1] He had a great desire for a poor girl who was a servant, and who worked for him. However, to win this girl he had to abandon his wife. So, he took his wife far into the woods to gather spruce-gum and then left her there.

She soon found out that she had lost her way and began wandering. She became more and more lost as she wandered for many days. At last, she came to a bear's den, and after entering, she found the chief of all the bears, who welcomed her, provided for her wants, and furnished her with pleasant food. However, but since the meat was raw, he went to a neighboring town for fire. Soon she began to live with him and was to him in all things as he wished, just like a wife.

As time went on, it came to pass that a newcomer was expected, and she asked the Bear to provide the baby's clothes. When the long-expected infant came, it was a boy, large, beautiful, and strong. He outdid all the other boys in everything.

And since the child was born in a strange way, he very soon displayed a magic power. No baby ever grew so rapidly. When he was just four months old, he wrestled with the Bear and threw him easily upon the floor.

---

1. This very singular legend was obtained for me from Mrs. W. Wallace Brown. It is from the Micmac and is in the original from beginning to end a song, or poem. For this reason I have given it a plain metrical form, neither prose nor poetry, such being quite the character of the original. But I have not introduced anything not in the original. [CGL]

Consequently, the mother saw that he would be a warrior, and the chief of other men. However, she loathed the life she led and wished to leave and live as she had done in days of old. But the Bear would in no way consent to this, and since her son was human, like herself, he loved his mother best and thought the way she did.

One day, he said to his mother, "Now I can wrestle well and throw the Bear as often as I choose. When I throw him on the ground next time, pick up a club. The rest is up to you."

They waited awhile until the son had grown so strong that the Bear was easily beaten. One day they wrestled as they always did, and then the woman, reinforced by hate and dying of desire for freedom and a better human life, gave the Bear such a vigorous blow that he fell down dead on the mossy floor.

Now they went their way back to the chieftain's town and found him married to the servant-girl. The mother was the only one who spoke, and the wild son tore down the wigwam of the Indian chief with just one blow. Then he called aloud unto the lightning in the sky above, "Come down to me and help me in my need! Build the most magnificent wigwam in the world. Build it, I say, and for my mother here!"

The lightning came, and with a single flash, it built the most beautiful wigwam a man has ever seen. And then, the son said, "Mother, I want to go and travel all over until I find another man who is as strong as I am. When I find him, I shall return to you."

So, he traveled far and wide, until he saw a man who lifted up a vast canoe with many people in it. This he did while raising it in the water. Then the man carried it ashore and lifted it on land.

Soon thereafter, the two agreed that they would move on together until they found a third equal to them in strength, if such a man existed somewhere in the world. They traveled by hill and lake and kept traveling until one day, far in a lonely land, they saw a man rolling a mighty rock, large as the largest wigwam, up a hill. But the Bear's son picked up the stone with ease threw it far over the mountain-top. Indeed, he threw it far beyond the rocky range. They heard it thunder down the depths below.

Then the three strong men went to hunt the moose. The one who had carried the ship remained in camp to do the cooking, while the others went with bow and spear far away to find their game.

Now when the sun was at the edge of noon, just balancing to fall, a boy came. He was a little wretched, elfish-looking child, as sad and sickly as a boy could be. He asked the man for food, and the strong man answered him, "Poor little fellow! There, the pot is full of venison, so go and eat your fill."

Indeed, he ate the dinner for the three of them. When he had done, he did not leave a scrap. Then he walked into the stony mountainside, as any man might walk into the fog, and in a second he was no more to be seen.

Now, when the two returned and heard the tale, they were right angry, especially since they were hungry men. The man who rolled the stone stayed next in turn, but when the little fellow came to him, he seemed so famished and shed such tears that this one also gave him permission to eat. Then, in a single swallow, as it seemed, he bolted all the food and yelled aloud with an insulting laugh. The man was enraged and grabbed him by the throat, but the strange boy tossed him off him as one would throw a nut and vanished into the mountain as before.

On the third day the mighty man himself remained at home, and soon the starveling child came and began to beg for food with tears.

"Eat," said the chief, "as other people eat, and no more tricks, or I will deal with you."

But he acted just as he had done the day before: he swallowed all the meat with the same jeering yell. Then the strong man attacked the boy. It was an awful battle; they fought together from the early morn until the sun went down, and then the elf—for elf he was—cried out, "I give in now!"

So, both his arms were tightly bound behind, and the strong man kept his prey tied by a long, tough cord of plaited hide, and the lariat was fastened with a noose around his neck. The elf walked in advance of the strong man, who followed behind, holding the cord well twisted around his hand. And so, they went into the mountainside and continued walking a long and winding way, down into a deep cavern, onward for many a mile. The light of sorcery shining from the elf made it all clear until at last the guide stopped in his course, and said: "Now listen to me. I am the servant of a frightful fiend, a seven-headed devil, whom I deemed no man could ever conquer, he and I being of equal strength. But I believe that you might conquer him, since I have found by bitter proof that you can conquer me. Here is a staff, the only thing on earth that man may use to smite him and give him pain. Now, do your best. It doesn't matter to me which one of you wins. One of you will be slain in what I think will be a roaring fight."

In came the evil creature with a scream and clutched the Indian with teeth and claws. There, in the magic cavern, many a mile from the sun's rays, they fought for seven days, the stubborn devil and the stubborn man, whose savage temper gave him fresher strength with every fresh wound. The more his blood ran from his body, all the more his heart grew harder with the love of fight, until he cut off the monster's seven heads. Consequently, he slew him, and the elf burst into laughter at the victory.

"Now," said the elf, "I have a gift for you. I have three sisters. They are all beautiful, and all of them will be your own if you will only untie my hands."

The strong man set him free. And so, the elf led the man to another cave, and there the strong man saw three girls so strangely fair they seemed to be a dream. The first, indeed, was very beautiful, and yet as plump as she was lovely; then the second maid was tall, superb, and most magnificent, in rarest furs, with richest wampum bands, the very picture of a perfect bride; but fairer than them both, much fairer than swans, which outrival ducks, the youngest smiled. And the young chieftain chose her for his own.

Now he went into daylight with the three girls. Far on the rocks above him he could see his two companions, and a sudden thought came to his mind, for he was quick to think; and so, he called to them: "I say, let down a rope. I have three girls here, and they cannot climb."

And so, the two strong men let down a rope. Then the first fairy-maid was raised by it, and then the second. Now the chief cried out: "It is my turn; now you must pull me up!"

Upon saying this, he tied a heavy stone, just his own weight, onto the long rope's end, and then told them to haul him up. The rope rose, but as it came just to the top, the traitors let it fall, as he supposed they would, to murder him. And then the chieftain said to the elf, "You know the mountain and its winding ways. Carry me on your back, and take me quickly to where those fellows are!"

The goblin flew, and in an instant, he was by their side and found the villains in a deadly fight, quarreling over the maids. But when they saw him, they ceased to wrestle, whereupon he said, "I risked my life to bring these girls out of the cavern, and I would have given each of you a wife. But you would have murdered me for doing all this. Now I could kill you, and you both deserve death at the stake, vile serpents that you are! Well, take your lives—you are too low for me—and with them take these two women, if they wish to wed with such incarnate brutes like you!"

Then, the two men went their way, and the women followed them along the forest forever and ever. They do not return anymore into this story. And then the strong man said to his young bride, "I must return to my village. Then I'll come again to fetch you. Wait for me here."

However, the woman, born from elfin magic, replied, "I warn you about a single thing. When you are once again at your wigwam door, a small black dog will leap to lick your hand. Beware, I say, for if he succeeds, you will surely forget me forever."

As she predicted, so it came to pass. And consequently, she waited in the lonely wood beside the mountain until a month went by, and then she arose and went to seek her love. It was early dawn when she reached the town and found the wigwam of the Sagamore. She sought a nearby hiding-place, where she might watch unseen, and found a tree, a broad old ash, which spread its winged boughs over the surface of a silent pool.

An old black Indian had a hut close by. When his daughter returned, she looked into the spring and saw a lovely face. The simple girl thought it was hers, her own face grown beautiful by sorcery which hung about the place. She threw away her pail and said, "Aha! I'll work no more. Some chief will marry me!" and so she went to smile among the men.

Then the girl's mother came, and she, too, beheld the same sweet, smiling, girlish face.

"Now I am young and beautiful again. I'll seek another husband, and I'll do this at once."

She threw her pail far away and went off, losing no time to smile among the men. And then, in turn, the old Indian came, and after looking in the spring, he beheld the face. He knew right away that it was not his own, for in his youth he never had been fair. So, looking up above, he saw the bride and asked her to come down to him. Then he said, "My wife has gone away; my daughter, too. You were the cause of it. Now it is but right that you take the place my wife has left. Therefore, remain with me and be my own."

He fares but ill who weds an unwilling witch. When night arrived, they laid themselves down to sleep, and then the bride murmured a magic prayer, begging the awful Spirit of the Wind, the giant Eagle of the wilderness, to do his worst. All at once, a fearful tempest blew, and all night long the old Indian was outside, working with all his might to keep the lodge from being blown away. As soon as he had pinned one sheet of bark into its place, another blew away, and then a tent pole rattling in the rain bounded afar. It was exhausting work, but all night long the young bride slept in peace, until the morning came, and then he slept.

Then she arose, and, after walking to the woods, she sat down beside a stream and sang a song:

"There are many men in the world,
But only one is dear to me.
He is good and brave and strong.
He swore to love none but me.
Yes, now he has forgotten me.
Deceived by sorcery very grim,
But I will love none but him."

And as she sat and sang, the Sagamore her husband came paddling by in his canoe and heard the sweet song intoned in magic style. All at once, he recalled what he had forgotten—the two strong giants, the cavern and the elf, the seven-headed monster and the fight, the sisters and the evil-minded men, and the black dog who leaped to lick his hand. All this flashed upon him like some early dream brought out by sorcery. He saw her sitting beside the stream, and still he heard her song, soft as a magic flute. He went to her, and in a minute he was won again.

And then she said, "This world is completely false. I know another. Let us go to it."

So, then again, she sang a magic spell, and as she sang, they saw the great Culloo, the giant bird, broad as a thunder cloud, winging his way towards them. When he arrived, they climbed on top of him, and he soared away. But to this earth they never came again.

Florentine Tales
and Legends

The Devil of the Old Market, or The Devil of the Palace Cavolaia

ON THE CORNER OF the Palace Cavolaia there were four devils of iron made many years ago. These were once four gentlemen who had been wonderfully intimate and had made a strange compact, swearing fidelity and love among themselves to death and agreeing also that if they married, their wives and children and property should be all in common.

When such vows and oaths are uttered, the saints may ignore them, but the devils hear them. Indeed, they hear them in hell, and they laugh and cry, "These are men who will some day be like us and will be here forever!"

Such a sin as this is like a root which, once planted, may be left alone—the longer it is in the ground, the more it grows. Earth does not spoil gold, but even virtue, like friendship, may grow into a great vice when it grows too much, as it happened in this case.

Well, the four friends were invited to a great party in that fatal palace of the Cavolaia, and they all went. While there, they danced and amused themselves. The four were all singularly handsome, the ladies came in their best array and made themselves appear magnificent so they would be courted by these gentlemen, and so they looked at one another with jealous eyes. Indeed, many a young woman there would have gladly been wife to them all, or wished that the four were one, while the married dames wished that they could be loved by one or all. People were wicked in those days!

But what was their surprise—and a fearful surprise it was—when, after all their gaiety, they heard at three o'clock in the morning the sound of a bell which they had never heard before, and then divine music and singing. All at once, a lady of such superhuman beauty entered and held them enchanted and speechless. Now it was known by the strict rules of that palace, the party had to close soon, and there was only time for one more dance, and the friends had sworn that every lady who danced with one of them had to dance with all in succession. Truly, they now repented their oath, for the unknown lady was so beautiful.

As the lady advanced, she pointed out one of the four and said, "I will dance with him alone."

The young signore would have refused, but he felt himself obliged to obey her despite himself, and after they had danced, she suddenly disappeared, leaving everyone amazed.

And when they had recovered from the spell which had been cast upon them, they said that as she had come in with the dawn and vanished with the day, it must have been the Beautiful Alba, the enchanting queen of the fairies.[1]

The festival lasted for three days, and every night at the same hour, the beautiful Alba reappeared, enchanting everyone so wonderfully that even the ladies forgot their jealousy and were just as much fascinated by her as were the men.

Now, of the four friends, three sternly reproached the other for breaking his oath, for they themselves were madly in love. However, he replied, and truly, that he had been compelled by some power which he could not resist to obey her. But that, as a man of honor, he would comply with the common oath that bound them so far as he could.

Then they declared that he should ask her if she loved him, and if she assented, that he should inform her of their oath, and that she must share her love with all or none which he did in good faith, and she answered: "If you had loved me sincerely and fully, you would have broken that vile oath, and yet, it is to your credit that, as a man of honor, you refuse to break your word. Therefore, you will be mine, but not until you endure a long and bitter

---

1. Alba is related to Bellaria, the Etruscan goddess or fairy. Leland based one of his books on this mysterious fairy, *The Book of One Hundred Riddles of the Fairy Bellaria*. [JZ]

punishment. Now, I ask your friends and you, if to be mine, they are willing to take the form of demons and bear it openly before all men."

And when he proposed it to his friends, he found them so madly in love with the lady that they declared that, to be hers, they would willingly wear any form, however terrible, thinking that she had meant some disguise.

Since they had never heard of such a punishment, they gazed at her in astonishment. But she replied, "Go into the street, and your feet will guide you, and truly it will be a great surprise."

Then they laughed among themselves and said, "The surprise will be that she will consent to become a wife to us all."

However, when they came to the corner that night, they were amazed to see four figures of devils and Alba, who said, "Now you are indeed mine, but as for my being yours, that is another matter."

Then touching each one, she also touched a devil, and said, "This is your form. Enter into it. Three of you will remain as such forever. As for this fourth young man, he will be with you for a year, and then, he will be set free and will live with me in human form. And from midnight until three in the morning, you also may be as you were, and go to the Palazzo Cavolaia, and dance and be merry with the rest of the people. But during the day you will become devils again."

And so, it came to pass. After a year the image of the chosen lover disappeared, and then one of the three was stolen, and then another, until only one remained.

There is some confusion in the conclusion of this story, which I have sought to correct. The exact words are, "For many years all four remained until one was stolen away, and that was the image of the young man who pleased the beautiful Alba, who thus relieved him of the spell." But since there has been always only one devil on the corner, I cannot otherwise reconcile the story with the fact.

The Enchanted Cow in La Via Vacchereccia

On Dunmore Heath I also slewe
A monstrous wild and cruel beaste
Called the Dun Cow of Dunmore plaine,
Who many people had opprest.

—Guy, Earl of Warwick

THE VIA VACCHERECCIA IS a very short street leading from the Signoria to the Via Por San Maria. *Vaccherrcia*, also *Vacchereccia*, means a cow, and is also applied scornfully to a bad woman. The following legend was given to me as accounting for the name of the place. A well-known Vienna beerhouse-restaurant, Gilli and Letta's, has contributed much of late years to make this street known, and it was on its site that, at some time in "the fabled past," the building stood in which dwelt the witch who figures in the story.

LONG AGO A POOR girl lived in the Via Vacchereccia. No matter how beautiful and graceful, and sweet she was, it seemed, however, to be a miracle that she belonged to the people, and even more, that she was the daughter of the woman who was believed to be her mother, for the latter was as ugly as she was wicked, brutal, and cruel before all the world, and a witch in secret, a creature without heart or humanity. Nor was the beautiful Artemisia—such being the name of the girl—in reality her daughter, for the old woman had stolen her from her parents, who were noble and wealthy, when she was a babe, and had brought her up, hoping that when grown she could make money out of her in some evil way, and live off her. But, as sometimes happens, it seemed as if some benevolent power watched over the poor child, for all the evil words and worse example of the witch had no effect on her whatsoever.

Now it happened that Artemisia in time attracted the attention and love of a young gentleman, who, while of moderate means, was by no means rich. He had learned to know her through his mother, an admirable lady, who had often employed Artemisia and been impressed by her beauty and goodness. Consequently, it happened that the mother favored the son's suit, and as Artemisia loved the young man, it seemed as if her sufferings would soon be at an end, for it should be known that the witch treated the maid at all times with extraordinary cruelty. But it did not suit the views of the old woman at all that the girl on whom she reckoned to bring in much money from great protectors, and whom she was wont to call the cow from whom she would yet draw support, should settle down as the wife of a small nobleman of moderate means. Consequently, she not only scornfully rejected the suit, but scolded and beat Artemisia with even greater wickedness than ever.

However, there are times when the gentlest natures (especially when supported by good principles and truly good blood) will not give way to any oppression, however cruel, and Artemisia, feeling keenly that the marriage was most advantageous for her, and a great honor, and that her whole heart had been wisely given, turned for once on the old woman and defied her. Indeed, she threatened to appeal to the law and showed that she knew so much that was wicked in her life that the witch became just as much frightened as she was enraged, knowing full well that an investigation by justice would bring her to the bonfire. So, inspired by the devil, she turned the girl into a cow and shut her up in a stable in the courtyard of the house, where she went every day two or three times to beat and torture her victim in the most fiendish manner.

Meanwhile the disappearance of Artemisia had excited much talk and suspicion since it followed immediately after the refusal of the old woman to give her daughter to the young gentleman. And he, indeed, was in sad shape and great suffering, but after a while, once he recovered, he began to wonder whether the maid was perhaps confined in the Via Vacchereccia. And as love doubles all our senses and makes the deaf hear, and, according to the proverb, "he who finds it in his heart will feel spurs in his flanks," so once this young man heard that people had spoken of the old woman as a witch, he began to wonder whether she might not be one in truth, and whether Artemisia might have been confined or enchanted into some form of an animal, and so imprisoned.

So, full of this thought one night, he went to the house, where there was an opening like a window or portal in the courtyard, and began to sing:

> Midnight is striking, I hear it afar,
> High in the heaven shines many a star.
> And oh that the voice of the one I could hear,
> Who suffers so sadly—the love I hold dear.
> Oh stars, if you're looking with pity on me,
> I pray you the maid from affliction to free!

As he sang this, he heard a cow lowing in the courtyard, and as his mind was full of the idea of enchantment, his attention was attracted to it. Then he sang:

> If enchanted here you be,
> Low, but gently, *one, two, three!*
> Low in answer unto me,
> And a rescue soon you'll see.

Then the cow lowed three times, very softly, and the young man was delighted, put to her other questions, and being very shrewd, he managed to extract with only yea and nay the entire story. Having learned all this, he reflected that to beat a terrier 'tis well to take a bulldog, and after much inquiry, he found that a great sorcerer was living in Arezzo, a man of noble character. Moreover, he was astonished to learn from his mother that this *gran mago* had been a friend of his father. So, after he was well received by the wise man, and having told his story, the sage replied:

"Evil indeed is the woman of whom you speak—a black witch of low degree, who has been allowed, as all of her kind are, to complete her measure of sin, in order that she may receive her full measure of punishment. For all things may be forgiven, but not cruelty, and she has lived on the sufferings of others. Yet, her power is of a petty kind, and such as any priest can crush. So, when she is absent, go to the stable. Indeed, I shall make sure that she will be away all tomorrow. Then bind verbena on the cow's horns, and hang a crucifix over the door, and sprinkle all the floor with holy water and incense, and sing to the cow:

'The witch is not your mother in truth,
She stole you in your early youth,
She has deserved your bitterest hate,
Then fear not to retaliate;
And when she comes to you again,
Then rush at her with might and main;
She has heaped on you many a scorn,
Repay it with your pointed horn.'

"And note that there is a halter on the cow's neck, and this is the charm which gives her the form of a cow, but it cannot be removed except in a church by the priest."

And he added other advice to this that was duly followed.

Then the next day the young man went to the stable and did all that the wise man had advised. So, he hid nearby and awaited the return of the witch. Indeed, he did not have long to wait, for the witch, who was evidently in a great rage at something, and bore a cruel-looking stick with an iron goad on the end, rushed to the courtyard and into the stable, but fell flat on the floor, overcome by the holy water. Then the cow, whose halter had been untied from the post, turned on her with fury, and tossed and gored her. She trampled on the witch until she was senseless. Then the cow ran full speed, guided by the young man, to the Baptistery, where there a priest was waiting for her. And the priest sprinkled her with holy water and took the halter from her neck. All at once, she was disenchanted and became once more the beautiful Artemisia.

When this was done, the young man took the halter, hurried back to the stable, and put it around the witch's neck. All at once, she became a cow without horns, or such which are called "the devil's own." Maddened with rage, she rushed forth, attacking everybody, causing the entire town to chase after her with staves, pikes, and all their dogs, and so they hunted her down through the Uffizi and along Lung' Arno, all roaring and screaming and barking, out into the country, for she gave them a long run and a good chase, until they came to a gate of a farm, over which was a Saint Antony, who, indignant that she dared pass under him, descended from his niche, and gave her a tremendous blow with his staff between the horns, or where they would have been if she had possessed them. Then the earth opened and swallowed her up, amid a fearful flashing of fire, and a smell which was even worse than that of the streets of Siena in summer-time which is often so fearful that the poorer natives commonly carry fennel (as people do perfumed vinaigrettes in other places) to sniff at, as a relief from the horrible odor.

When all this was done, the sorcerer revealed to the maiden that her parents, who were still living, were very great and wealthy people, so that there was soon a grand reunion, a general recognition, and a happy marriage.

> Maidens, beware lest witches catch you!
> Think of the Via Vacchereccia;
> And tourists dining in the same,
> Note how the street once got its name.

La Fortuna

One day Good Luck came to my home,
I begged of her to stay.
"There's no one loves you more than I,
Oh, rest with me for awhile."
"It may not be. It may not be.
I rest with no one long," said she.

— Witch Ballads by C. G. Leland

THE MANNER IN WHICH many of the gods in exile still live in Italy is very fully illustrated by the following story. It is a hard thing sometimes nowadays for a family to pass for noble if they are poor, or only poor relations. But it was easy in olden days, easy as drinking good Chianti. A signore had only to put his shield with something carved on it over his window, and he was all right. He was noble without a doubt. Now the nobles had their own noble stories as to what these noble pictures in stone meant, but the ignoble people often had another story just as good. Coarse woolen cloth wears as well as silk. Now you may see on an old palazzo in the Via de' Cerchi, and indeed, in several other places, a shield with three rings. But people call them three wheels. And this is the story about the three wheels.

There was once a very good man who lived in squalid misery. He had a wife and two children, one blind and another crippled, and both were ugly beyond telling! This poor man often wept out of despair, and then he would repeat:

"The wheel of Fortune turns, they say,
But for me it turns the other way.
I work with good-will, but do what I may,
I have only bad luck from day to day."

Yes, little to eat and less to wear, and two poor girls, one blind and one lame. People say that Fortune is blind herself and cannot walk, but she does not bless those who are like her. That is for sure! And so, he wailed and wept, till it was time to go forth to seek work to gain their daily bread. And a hard time he had of it.

Now it happened that very late one night, or very early one morning, as one might say, between dark and dawn, he went to the forest to cut wood. When having called to Fortune as was his wont, what was his surprise suddenly to see before his eyes a gleam of light, and as he raised his head, he beheld a lady of enchanting beauty passing along rapidly, not walking but on a rolling ball moving her limbs. I cannot say feet, for she had none. In place of them were two wheels, and these wheels, as they turned, threw off flowers that produced a delicious perfume.

The poor man uttered a sigh of relief upon seeing this and said: "Beautiful lady, believe me when I say that I have invoked you every day. You are the Lady of the Wheels of Fortune, and had I known how beautiful you are, I would have worshipped you for your beauty alone. Even your very name is beautiful to utter, though I have never been able to couple it with mine, for one may see that I am not one of the fortunate. Yet, though you are my enemy, give me, I pray, just a little of the luck which flies from your wheel! Do not believe, I pray, that I am envious of those who are your favorites, nor that because you are my enemy that I am yours, for if you do not deem that I am worthy, assuredly I do not deserve your grace, nor will I, like many, say that Fortune is not beautiful, for having seen you, I can now praise you more than ever."

"I do not cast my favors always on those who deserve them," replied Fortune, "so, this time my wheel will assist you. But tell me, man of honesty and without envy, which would you prefer—to be fortunate in all things yourself alone, or to give instead as much good luck to two men as miserable as you are? If you will gain the prize for yourself alone, turn and pluck one of these flowers! If for others, then take two."

The poor man replied: "It is far better, lady, to raise two families to prosperity than one.

"As for me, I can work, and thank God and you that I can do so much good to many, although I do not profit by it myself."

After saying this, he advanced and plucked two flowers while Fortune smiled.

"You must have heard," she said, "that when I spend, I am lavish and extravagant, and assuredly you know the saying that 'Three is the lucky number, or nine.' Now I make it a rule that when I relieve families, I always do it by threes. So do go and pluck a flower for yourself."

When the poor man heard this, he went to the wheels, and let them turn until a very large fine flower came forth, and he seized it. Immediately, Fortune smiled, and said: "I always favor the bold. Now go and sit on the bench over there until someone comes."

Upon saying this, she vanished. Then two very poor woodcutters whom he knew very well arrived. One had two sons, another a son and a daughter, one and all were as poor and miserable as could be.

"What has happened to you that has made you look so handsome and young," said one of the woodcutters who was amazed, as he approached.

"And what fine clothes," remarked the second.

"The same thing will soon happen to both of you," replied Fortune's favorite. "Just take these flowers and guard them well."

"Yes, Signore," they replied and sat down on the bench like three beggars, and they rose as three fine cavaliers, in velvet and satin, with gold mounted swords, and found their horses and attendants waiting. And when they arrived home, they did not know their wives or children, nor did they recognize them, and it was an hour before everything was straightened out. Then they all went with them as if it were their usual way of living. The first man found a great treasure the very first day in his cellar, and in short, they all grew rich, and the three sons married the three girls, and they all put the three wheels on their shields. One of the wheels is the ball on which Fortune rolled along, and the other two are her feet; or else the three men each took a wheel to himself. Anyhow, there they are, pick and choose. Let him who has brains, use them!

Now, there is a saying that "not every blossom bears a fruit," but the flowers of Fortune bear fruit enough to make up for the short crop elsewhere.

There is some sense and use in such stories as these. After all, a poor devil who half believes—and very often quite believes in them—gets a great deal of hope and comfort out of them. They make him trust that luck or fairies, or something, will give him a good turn yet some day, and so he hopes, and truly, as they say, "no pretty girl is ever quite poor, so no man who hopes is ever really broken."

The Goblin of La Via del Corno

THERE WAS IN WHAT is now known as the Via del Corno an ancient palace, which a long time ago was inhabited only by a certain gentleman and a goblin. He did not have any servants because those who visited his palace did not remain more than one day for fear of the goblin. And as this fear spread far and wide, people kept away from the Via del Corno after dark. But since this also kept away the thieves and since the goblin did all the housework, the master was all the more pleased. Only on one point did the two differ, and that was on the point of morality. Here the goblin was extremely strict and drew the line distinctly. Several times, as was the custom in those wicked days, the Signore attempted to introduce a lady-friend to the palazzo, but all night long, the goblin, when not busy in pulling the sheets from the fair sinner, was busily occupied in strewing nettles or burrs under her, or tickling the soles of her feet with a pen, and then soon, when, sinking to sleep, she hoped for some remission of the tease, he would begin to play interminable airs on a horn. It is true that he played beautifully, like no earthly musician, but even enchanting airs may be annoying when they prevent sleep.

Nor did the lord fare the better, even when, inspired by higher motives, he "would a-wooing go." Indeed, one lady or another had heard of the goblin, and when they had not, it always happened that by some mysterious means or other the match was broken off.

In the meantime the life led by the Signore was rather peculiar, as he slept nearly all day, sallied forth for an hour or two to exercise, go to a barber's, make his small purchases, or hear the news, supped at a trattoria, and then returning home, sat all night listening to the goblin as he played divinely on the horn, or blew it himself, which he did extremely well, drank an excessive amount of alcohol and hobnobbed with his familiar, who was a great critic of wine, and, as the proverb says, "Good wine, long tales"—they told one another no end of merry and marvelous stories, and since wine makes men sing, they also sang duets, solos, and glees. And when the weather was bad, chilly, rainy, or too hot, they cured it with Chianti, according to a medical prescription laid down in sundry rare old works,

> Cloudy sky in the morning early,
> What will make you vanish fairly?
> Ah! this goblet of good wine,
> Essence of the blessed vine,
> Shall be for you a medical sign!

Then they played chess, cards, cribbage, drole, ecart, Pope Joan, bo, brag, casino, thirty-one, put, snip-snap-snorem, lift-em-up, tear-the-rag, smoke, blind-hookey, bless-your-grandmother, Polish-bank, seven-up, beggar-my-neighbor, patience, old-maid, fright, baccarat, *belle-en-chemise*, bang-up, howling-Moses, bluff, swindle-Dick, go-it-rags, ombre or keep-dark, morelles, go-hang, goose, dominoes, loto, *morra* or push-pin. And when extra hands were needed, they came, but all that came were only fairy hands. Short at the wrist, the goblin would remark that it saved wine not to have mouths, *et cetera*. Then they had long and curious and exceedingly weighty debates as to the laws of the games and fair play, not forgetting meanwhile to sample all the various wines ever sung by Redi.[1] So they got on, the Signore realizing that one close friend is worth a hundred distant relations.

Now, one night it happened that the goblin, watching the Signore finish off a pint of good old strong Barolo very neatly and carefully, without taking breath or winking, exclaimed with a long, deep sigh:

---

1. Francesco Redi's poem, *Bacchus in Toscany*, is known even to the most ignorant in Florence because very cheap editions are constantly sold there. [CGL]

"You are a gallant fellow, a right true boon companion, and it grieves me to the heart to think that you are doomed to be drowned tomorrow."

"Oh, you're joking with me," replied the Signore. "There isn't water enough in the Arno now to drown a duck, unless it held its head under in a half-pint puddle."

The goblin went to the window, took a look at the stars, whistled and said: "As I expected, it is written that you are to be drowned tomorrow, unless you carry this horn of mine hung around your neck all day.

If you find yourself forlorn,
Blow aloud this little horn,
And you will be safe and sound,
For with it you'll not be drowned."

Upon saying this, the goblin solemnly handed the horn to the cavalier, drank a goblet of muscato, wiped his lips, bowed a ceremonious good-night, and, as was his wont, vanished with dignity up the chimney.

The gentleman was more troubled by this prediction than he liked to admit. I need not say that the next day he did not go near the Arno, though it was as dry as a bone. Indeed, he kept out of a bath and was almost afraid to wash his face. Finally, he imagined that some enemies or villains would burst into his lonely house, bind him hand and foot, carry him far away, and drown him in some isolated stream, or perhaps in the sea. He remembered just such a case. We all remember just such cases when we don't want to. That was it, decidedly.

Then he had a happy thought. There was a little hiding-chamber, centuries old, in the palazzo, known only to himself, with a concealed door. He would go and hide there. He shouted for joy, and when he entered the room, he leaped with a great bound from the threshold of the door, down and over three or four steps, into the middle of the little room.

Now he did not know that in the cellar below his hiding-place there was an immense vat, containing hundreds of barrels of wine, such as are used to hold the rough wine before it is drawn off and finished. Nor did he know that the floor was extremely decayed, so that when he landed on it with a bounce, it gave way, and he found himself in the cellar overhead and ears in wine. And, truly, for a minute he imagined in earnest that he was drowning. The sides of the vat were so high that he could not climb out. But while swimming and struggling for life, he reached for a nail in the side, and he held on to it, crying as loud as he could shout for aid But no one came, and he was just beginning to despair, when he thought of the horn!

It still hung around his neck, and so he poured out the wine and blew on it. All at once, there was a tremendous, appalling, and unearthly blast that he himself could never have blown. It rang far and wide all over Florence and was heard beyond Fiesole. It wakened the dead in old Etruscan graves, for an instant, to think they had been called by Tinia to meet the eleven gods. It caused all the goblins, fairies, demons, witches, and sorcerers to stop their deviltries or delights for an instant. In fact, it was the Great Blast of the Horn of the Fairies, which only plays second fiddle to the last trump.

And at that sound all Florence came running to see what the matter was. The Grand Duke and his household came; the Council of the Eight burst their bonds and left the Palazzo Vecchio. Everybody came, and they fished out the signore and listened with awe to his tale. The priests said that the goblin was San Zenobio, the more liberal swore it was Crescenzio, the people held to plain San Antonino. The signore became a great man.

"My son," said the goblin to him in confidence the following evening, as they sat over their wine, "this is our last night together. You are saved, and I have fulfilled my duty to you. Once I, too, was a man like you, and in that life you saved mine by rescuing me from assassins. And I swore to watch over you in every dangerous situation, and bring you to a happy end.

> The final hour has come for me.
> Street of the Horn, farewell to you!
> Farewell, Oh palace, farewell, Oh street!
> My lord, in another world we'll meet."

Then the goblin told the Signore that he would before long enter into a happy marriage, and this was the reason why he had kept him in the past from forming relationships which would have prevented it, and that, if in future he should ever be in great need of assistance, he was to blow the horn, and he would come to him, but that this must always be in the palace alone after midnight. Then, upon saying all this, he vanished.

The Signore grieved for a long time at the loss of his goblin friend, but he married happily, as had been predicted, and his life was long and prosperous. So, he put the horn in his shield, and you may see it to this day on the Church of Santa Maria Novella. And this was how the Via del Corno got its name.

The Imp of the Devil's Corner and the Pious Fairy

THERE WAS ONCE A pious fairy who employed all her time by going about the streets of Florence in the shape of a woman, preaching moral sermons for the good of her listeners, and singing so sweetly that everyone who heard her voice fell in love with her. Even the women forgot to be jealous. So charming was her voice that dames and damsels followed her about, trying to learn her manner of singing.

Now, the fairy had converted so many folk from their evil ways that a certain devil or imp—who also had much to do in Florence about that time—became jealous of the intruder, and swore to avenge himself. However, it appears that there was as much love as hate in the fiend's mind, for the fairy's beautiful voice had worked its charm even though the hearer was a devil.

Besides being an imp of superior intelligence, he was also an accomplished ventriloquist (or one who could imitate strange voices whether making sounds from far away or in any place). So, one day, while the pious fairy in the form of a beautiful maiden held forth to an admiring audience, two voices were heard on the street, one here, another there, and the first sang:

> "Hear, Oh lovely maid, a word,
> Only to you yourself I'd bear it,
> For it must not he overheard,
> Least of all should the preacher hear it.
> Know that, while seeming pious, she,

Holding in hand a rosary,

Her talk is all hypocrisy,

To make believe to simple ears,

That still the maiden wreath she wears."

Then another voice answered:

"Friends, you'll not have long to wait

For what I am going to relate.

And it is a pretty story

Which I am going to lay before you.

That dame who singing there you see

Is a witch of this our Tuscany,

Who up and down the city flies,

Deceiving people with her lies,

Saying to one: The truth to tell,

I know you love your husband well;

But you will find, on close inspection,

Another has his fond affection."

In short, the imp, by changing his voice artfully, and singing his ribald songs everywhere, managed in the end to persuade people that the fairy was no better than she should be, and was a common mischief-maker and disturber of domestic peace. Consequently, the husbands, who became jealous, began to quarrel with their wives and then to swear at the witch, who led them astray or put false suspicion into their minds.

But it happened that the fairy was favored highly by a great saint, and when she went to him, she told all her troubles and the wicked things which were said about her. Then she asked him to free her good name from the slanders which the imp of darkness had spread all over.

As a result, the saint became very angry and decided to change the imp into a bronze figure. But first he compelled the little devil to go to everyone who had been influenced by his slanders and undo the mischief which he had caused. Finally, he was to make a full public confession about everything, including his designs on the beautiful fairy, and how he hoped by compromising her to lead her to share his fate.

Truly, the imp cut but a sorry figure when compelled to stand up in the Old Market place at the corner of the Palazzo Cavolaia before a vast multitude and avow all his dirty little tricks. However, he contrived artfully to represent his passionate love for the fairy and to attribute all his sins to this love so that many had compassion for him. Indeed, soon people stopped speaking ill of the poor imp, for they said he was to be pitied because he had no love on earth and was shut out of heaven. Nor did he quite lose his power, for it was said that after he had been confined in the bronze image, if anyone poke ill of him or said, "This is a devil, and as a devil he can never enter Paradise," then the imp would persecute that man with strange voices and sounds until such time as the offender went to the Palazzo della Cavolaia, and stood before the bronze image to ask his pardon.

And if it pleased the imp, he forgave those who came, and they had peace. But if it did not, they were pursued by the double mocking voice which made dialogue or sang duets about all their sins and follies and disgraces. Whether these people stayed at home or went abroad, the voices stayed with them, crying loudly, tittering, whispering, or hissing, so that they had no rest day or night. And this is what happened to all those who spoke ill of the imp of the Devil's Corner.

Il Palazzo Feroni

SIGNORE PIETRO, WHO AFTERWARDS received the name Feroni, was a very rich man, and yet hated by the poor, on whom he bestowed nothing, and not much liked by his equals, though he provided them expensive entertainment. Indeed, there was something inconsistent and contradictory in the man and his character—"the horns against the cross," as the proverb has it, which made it so that one never knew where to place him:

> On the hill in joy, in the dale in sorrow.
> One thing today, and another to-morrow.

To consider him at every point, there was something to count off. Thus, in the entire city there was no one—according to his own declaration—who was:

> Richer or more prosperous,
> Or who had enjoyed a better education,
> Or who had such remarkable general knowledge of every-
> thing taking place,
> Or more of a distinguished courtier,
> Or one with such a train of dependents, and people of all
> kinds running after him,
> Or more generally accomplished,
> Or better looking.

And finally, no one so physically strong, as he was accustomed to boast to everybody on first acquaintance, and give them proof of it, for he had heard somewhere that "physical force makes a deeper impression than courtesy."

But all these fine gifts failed to inspire respect (and here was another puzzle in his nature), either because he was so tremendously vain that he looked down on all mortals as if they were insects, and all pretty much alike as compared to himself, or else from a foolish carelessness and want of respect, he made himself quite as familiar with trivial people as with anybody.

One evening Signore Pietro gave a grand ball in his palace, and as the guests entered—the beauty and grace and courtly style of all Italy in its golden time—he half closed his eyes, lazily looking at the brilliant swarm of human butterflies and walking flowers, despising while admiring them, though if he had been asked to give a reason for his contempt, he would have been puzzled, not having any great amount of self-respect for himself. And they spun round and round in the dance. . . .

All of a sudden, when he saw a lady, unknown to him of such striking and singular appearance among all the guests, he was promptly aroused from his idle thought. She was indeed wonderfully beautiful, but what was very noticeable was her absolutely ivory white complexion, which hardly seemed human, and her profuse black silken hair. Most of all, he was attracted to her unearthly large jet-black eyes. They were incredibly brilliant with such a strange expression that neither the Signore Pietro nor anyone else present had ever seen before. There was a power in them, a kind of basilisk-fascination allied to angelic sweetness—fire and ice . . . hot and cold wind.

Signore Pietro, with his prompt tact, made the lady's paleness a pretense for addressing her. "Did she feel ill—everything in the house was at her disposal—

> Servants, carpets, chairs and tables,
> Kitchen, pantry, hall and stables,
> Everything above or under,
> All my present earthly plunder,
> All too small for such a wonder."

The lady replied with a smile and a glance in which there was not the slightest trace of being startled or abashed:

"'Tis not worth while your house to rifle,

Oh mio Signor, for such a trifle,

'Tis but a slight indisposition,

For which rest, by your permission."

Since he liked to improvise, Signore Pietro was delighted with such a ready answer, and as he remarked that he was something of a doctor, he begged permission to bring a soothing cordial, admirable for the nerves, which he hoped to have the honor of placing directly in that fairy-like hand. . . . The Signore vanished to seek the soothing cordial.

By this time, the guests had begun to notice this lady, and due to her extremely strange appearance, they gathered around her, expecting at first to have some sport in listening to, or quizzing an eccentric or a character. But they changed their mind when they came to consider her—some feeling an awe as if she were a fairy, and everyone convinced that, whoever she was, she had come there to sell somebody amazingly cheap, nor did they feel quite assured that they themselves were not included in the bargain.

Soon Signore Pietro returned with the soothing cordial. He had evidently not drunk any of it himself while on the errand, for there was a massive chased iron table inlaid with gold and silver in his way, and with an angry blow from his giant arm, like one from a blacksmith's hammer, the mighty lord broke it and knocked it over. Flirtation had begun.

"Did you hurt yourself, Signore?" the lady amiably asked.

"Not I, indeed," he replied proudly. "Stone is my name, but it ought to have been Iron, lady, for I am hard as nails, a regular Ferrone or big man of iron, and all my ancestors were Ferroni, too. Ah, we are a strong lot—at your service!"

Saying this, he handed the cup to the lady, who drank the potion, and then, instead of giving the goblet back to Signore Pietro, as he expected, meaning to gallantly drink the rest of the sweet cordial, she beckoned with her finger and an upward scoop of her hand to the table, which was lying disconsolately on its back with its legs upwards, like a trussed chicken waiting to be carved, when suddenly, at the signal, it jumped up and came walking to her like a Christian, its legs moving most humanly, and yet all present were appalled at the sight, and the Signore gasped, "I believe the devil's in it!"

Meanwhile, the lady calmly placed the drink on the table and smiled benevolently. There was something in that angelic smile which made the Signore feel as if he had been made into game. Enraged, he rushed toward the table, which reared up on its hind legs and showed it was ready to fight with its forepaws, on which there were massy round iron balls, as on the other extremities. Truly, it was a desperate battle, and both combatants covered themselves with dust and glory. Now the table would put a ball well in, and the Signore would counter, or, as I may say, cannon or cannon-ball it off; and then they would grapple and roll over and over until the Signora called time out. At last, the lord wrenched all the cannon-balls off the table, which first, making a jump to the ceiling, came down in its usual position, while the balls began dancing on it like mad.

All present roared with laughter at such a sight, and it was observed that the lady, no longer pale, flushed with merriment like a rose. As for Signore Pietro, he was red as a beet, and sighed that he had been mocked or quizzed.

"Truly yes," the lady replied, "but from now on, you will have a name, for to do you justice, you are as hard as iron, and Iron you shall be called—Big Iron Ferrone—and cannonballs will be your coat-of-arms by edict of the Queen of the Fairies!"

Now, upon hearing this, all the love in Signore Pietro became concentrated in his heart, passed into his tongue, and caused him to burst forth in song in the following octave, while the music accompanied:

> "When I behold your all too lovely features,
> I feel my heart in soft convulsions heaving,
> You are the most entrancing of all creatures,
> I tell you so in truth, without deceiving,
> In fact there is no beauty which can beat yours.
> And Pietro loves you, lady, past believing.
> In breasts like cannon-balls there's nothing to blame.
> But oh! I hope your heart's not like the same!"

But as this exquisite song concluded with an immense sigh, there appeared before them a golden and pearl carriage, which the fairy entered. Then it rose and sailed away through a great hole in the ceiling, which opened and closed behind her. Signore Pietro could do nothing but gape with opened jaws until it was all over.

"Well!" exclaimed the master. "She gave me the slip, but we have had a jolly evening of it, and I'm the first man who ever fought an iron table, and I've got a good idea. My name is now Feroni—the Big Iron Man—ladies and gentlemen, please remember, and cannon-balls are in my coat-of-arms!'"

I have naturally taken some liberty as regards mere text in translating this tale, in order to render the better the spirit of the original; but not so much as may be supposed, and spirit and words are, on the whole, accurately rendered.

The reader is not to suppose that there are any traces of true history in this fairy tale. I am very greatly indebted to Miss Wyndham of Florence (who has herself made collections in folk-lore), for investigating this subject of the Feroni family, with the following result—it being premised that it had occurred to the lady that the "cannon-balls" or Medicean pills, or pawnbroker's sign, whatever it was, had been attributed by mistake to the Feroni. Miss Wyndham, after consulting with authority, found that the Feroni themselves had not the balls, but, owing probably to transfer of property, there is found on their palaces the Alessandri shield, on which the upper half and lower left quarter contain the Medici spheres. She also sent me this extract from the old work, *Marietta di Ricci*:

> "The Feroni family, originally named from Balducci da Vinci, and of peasant origin, owes its fortune to Francesco, son of Baldo di Paolo di Ferone, a dyer of Empoli. Going as a merchant to Holland, he accumulated a large fortune. Made known to Cosimo III (just called to the Grand Duchy) by his travels, he was called to Florence. In 1673 he was made citizen of Florence, in 1674 he was elected senator, and in 1681 appointed Marquis of Bellavista. He left a colossal fortune, which has been

kept up by his heirs to the present day. His grandson Giuseppe was made cardinal in 1753.

"Their arms are an arm mailed in iron, holding a sword, and above it a golden lily in a blue field."

This extract is interesting, as showing how a family could rise by industry and wealth, even in one generation, by the work of a single man, to the highest honors in Florence. And it is very remarkable that some impression of the origin of this vigorous artisan and merchant, of peasant stock, is evident in the tale.

The Two Fairies of the Well

When looking down into a well,
You'll see a fairy, so they tell,
Although she constantly appears
With your own face instead of hers.
And if you cry aloud, you'll hear
Her voice soaring from the well.
Her ringing echo is quite clear.
Thus every one unto himself
May be a fairy, or an elf.[1]

LONG AFTER CHRISTIANITY HAD arrived and dominated Europe, there were many places in the vast edifice of society which the old heathen deities refused to leave, and there are even yet nooks and crannies in the mountains where they receive a kind of sorcerer's worship as elves. A trace of this lingering in a faith outworn, in nymphs, dryads, and fairies, can be found in the following story.

There once lived in Florence a young nobleman, who had grown up putting great faith in fairies, nymphs, and similar spirits, believing that they were friendly and brought good fortune to those who showed them respect. Now there was in his palazzo in the Via Calzaioli, at the corner of the Condotta, a very old well or fountain, on which were ancient and worn images,

---

1. "And truly those nymphs and fairies who inhabit wells, or are found in springs and fountains, can predict or know what is to take place, as may be read in Pausanias, and this power they derive from their *habitat*, or, as Creuzer declares (*Symbolik*, part iv. 72), they are called Muses, inasmuch as they dwell in Hippocrene and Aganippe, the inspiring springs of the Muses."—*On the Mysteries of Water*. FRIEDRICH (*Symbolik*). [CGL]

and in which there was a marvelous echo, and it was said that two nymphs had their home in it. And the Signore, believing in them, often cast wine or flowers into the spring, uttering a prayer to them, and at table he would always cast a little wine into water, or sprinkle water on the ground to do them honor.

One day he was dining with two friends, and they ridiculed him when he did this, and still more when he sang a song praising nymphs and fairies in answer to their remarks. Consequently, one said to him:

> Truly, I would like to see
> An example, if it may be,
> How a fairy in a fountain,
> Or a goblin of the mountain,
> Or a nymph of stream or wood,
> Ever did one any good,
> For such fays of air or river,
> One might wait, I think, forever,
> And if even such things be,
> They are devils all to me.

Somewhat angered by this remark, the young Signore replied:

> In the wood and by the stream,
> Not in reverie or in dream,
> Where the ancient oak-trees blow,
> And the murmuring torrents flow,
> Men whose wisdom none condemn
> Oft have met and talked with them.
> Demons for you they may be,
> But are angels unto me.

To which his friend sang in reply, laughing:

> Only prove that they exist,
> And we will no more resist.

Let them come before we go,
With *ha! ha! ha! and ho! ho! ho!*

And as they sang this, they heard a peal of silvery laughter outside, or, as it seemed, actually singing in the hall and making a chorus with their voices. And at that very instant a servant came and said that two very beautiful ladies were outside and begged the young Signore to come to them immediately, and that it was on a matter of life and death.

So he rose and stepped outside, but he had hardly crossed the threshold before the stone ceiling of the hall collapsed with a tremendous crash, and just where the young Signore had sat there was a great stone weighing many hundreds of pounds, so that it was plain that if he had not been called away just at that moment, he would have been crushed like a fly under a hammer. As for his two friends, they had broken arms and cut faces, bearing marks in memory of that day to the end of their lives.

When the young Signore was outside and looked for the ladies, they were gone, and a little boy, who was the only person present, declared that he had seen them, and that they were wonderfully beautiful, and that they had jumped or gone down into the well merrily laughing.

Therefore, it was generally believed by all who heard the tale that it was the Fairies of the Well, who thus saved the life of the young Signore. So, from that day he honored them more devoutly than ever; nor did his friends any longer doubt that there are spirits of air or earth, who, when treated with pious reverence, can confer benefits on their worshippers.

> For there are fairies all around
> Everywhere, and elves abound,
> Even in our homes unseen.
> They go wherever we have been,
> And often by the fireside sit,
> Laughing gaily at our wit.
> And when the ringing echo falls
> Back from the ceiling or the walls,
> 'Tis not our voices to us thrown

In a reflection, but their own;
For they are near at every turn,
As he who watches soon may learn.

And since they had saved his life, the young Signore honored the fairies by putting them on the sides of his coat-of-arms, as you may see by the shield which is on the house at the corner of the Via Calzaioli.

How La Via della Mosca Got Its Name

THIS IS THE WAY that the Via della Mosca, or the Street of the Fly, got its name. There once was a very old house on this street, and in this house was a family which, while of rank, was not very wealthy. Therefore, the members of this family lived in a modest manner. There were father, mother, and one daughter, who was wonderfully beautiful—true sunshine.

And since the sun has its shadow, so there was a living darkness in this family in the form of a servant woman who had been with them many years. She had a daughter of her own, who was also a beauty of a kind, but as dark as the other was fair. The two were like day and night, and just as they differed in face, they were also unlike in soul. The young signora did not have a fault in her. She would not have caused anyone pain even to have her own way or please her vanity, and they say the devil would drop dead if ever he were to meet with such a woman as *that*. However, he never met with this young lady, I suppose, because he is still living. And the young lady was so gentle of heart that she never said an ill word of anyone, while the maid and her mother never opened their mouths, save for gossip and slander. In contrast, the young signora was so occupied with constant charity, caring for poor children, and finding work for poor people that she never thought about her own beauty at all, and when people told her that "Whoever is born pretty is born to be wed," she would reply, "Pretty or ugly, there are things more important in life than weddings."

And she meant very much what she said so that she gave no heed at all to a very gallant and handsome yet good-hearted, honorable, wealthy young gentleman, who lived in a palazzo opposite hers, and who had fallen desperately in love with her by watching and admiring her. So, he made a proposal of marriage to her through her parents, but she replied (because her mind, in truth, had been on other things) that she was too much taken up with other duties to properly care for a husband, and that her dowry was not sufficient to correspond to his wealth, however generous he might be in dispensing with one. And since she was as firm and determined as she was gentle and good, she resolutely kept him at arm's length. But firmness is nothing against fate, and in the war of love, whoever flees, wins.

Now, if she was indifferent to the young signore, the dark maid-servant was not, for she had fallen as much in love with him as an evil, selfish nature would permit her, and she planned and plotted with her mother by night and by day to bring about what she desired. Now, unknown to all, the old woman was a witch, as all wicked women really are—they rot away with vanity and self-will and evil feelings until their hearts are like tinder or gunpowder, and then one day a spark of the devil's fire comes, and they flash out into witches of some kind.

Now, the young signore had a great love for boating on the Arno, which was a deeper river in those days. He would often pass half the night in his boat, and the mother and daughter managed to arrange things so that the young signorina would return very late on a certain night from visiting the poor accompanied by the old woman. And when they were just in the middle of the bridge, Ponte Vecchio, the mother gave a whistle, and suddenly, there was a sudden and terrible blast of wind, which blew the young lady into the air and whirled her over the bridge into the rushing river beneath the bridge.

But, as fate would have it, the young man was in his boat just below.

And fortune shone upon him, as it were, from heaven. Once he saw a form float or flit past him in the water and darkness, he lunged at it and drew it into the boat, and truly Pilate's wife was not so astonished when the roast capon rose up in the dish and crowed as was this boatman at finding what he had fished up out of the river.

Now, there is a saying about a very unlucky, contrary sort of man who, when he fell into the Arno, he burnt himself. But in this case, by luck, the falling of the young lady into the river caused her heart to burn with love because the young signore behaved so bravely, courteously, and kindly.

Indeed, he brought her home promptly without a sign of love-making or hint of the past so that she began to reconsider her refusal. As a result, it all ended with the signorina agreeing to wed the young man, and this caused the mother and daughter to become completely enraged when they saw how they had only hastened and aided what they had tried to prevent.

Of course, it is true that bad people put ten times as much strong will and hard work into their evil acts than good folk do into better deeds, because the latter think their cause will help itself along, while the sinners know perfectly well that they must help themselves or lose. So, the witch only persevered all the more, and at last she hit on a new plan. With much devilish ado she enchanted a comb of thorns so that whoever was combed with it would turn into a fly and had to remain one until the witch allowed the victim to assume his or her usual form.

Then on the bridal morn the old woman offered to comb out the long golden locks of the young lady, and since no other person was present, the witch began her incantation:

> Earthly beauty fade away,
> Maiden's form no longer stay,
> For a fly you will become,
> And as a busy insect hum,
> *Hum—hum—brum—brum*!
> *Buzz-uz-uz* around the room!
>
> Open your eyes and spread your wings,
> Pass away to insect things.
> Now the world will hate you more
> Than it ever loved before
> When it hears your ceaseless hum,
> *Buzz-uz-uz* around the room!

Upon hearing this, the bride sank into a deep sleep, during which she changed into a fly and soared up to the ceiling and around the room, all the time, buzzing and buzzing.

Now, with all her cleverness, the witch had missed a stitch in her sorcery, for she had not combed hard enough to draw blood, being afraid to wake the maiden. Consequently, it came to pass that, instead of a small common fly, she became a very large and exquisitely beautiful one with a head like gold, a silver body, and beautiful blue and silver wings like her bridal dress. And she was not confined to buzzing, for she had the power to sing one verse. However, when the change took place, the old woman rushed from the room screaming like mad, and declaring that her young mistress was a witch who had turned into a fly as soon as she had touched her with a consecrated comb which had been dipped in holy water. To all this she added many lies. For instance, she asserted that to avoid the holy sacrament of marriage a witch always changed her form, and that she had always suspected the signorina of being a witch ever since she had seen her fly in the wind over the Arno to the young signore.

But when the people went to look at the fly and found it so large and beautiful, they were amazed and also astonished when they heard it begin to buzz with a most entrancing strangely sweet sound and then sing:

> Don't be amazed that I
> Am enchanted as a fly.
> Evil witchcraft was around me,
> Evil witches' spells have bound me.
> Now I am a fly I know,
> But woe to her who made me so!

And when the young signore stretched out his hand, the fly came buzzing with joy and landed like a bird on his finger. She did this with great joy whenever any of the poor whom she had befriended came to see her, and so she behaved to all whom she had loved. And when it was observed that the fly had no fear of holy things, but seemed to love them, everyone believed her song.

Then, one day the young signore called all the family and friends together and said, "It is certainly true that the woman who was to have been my wife has been turned into a fly. And as for her being a witch, you can all see that she fears neither holy water nor a crucifix. But I believe that these women here, her nurse and daughter, have filled our ears with lies, and that the nurse herself is the sorceress who has done the evil deed. Now, I propose that we take all three, the fly, the mother, and daughter, and hang the room with verbena, which I have provided, and sprinkle the three with much holy water, all of us making the *castagna* and *jettatura*, and see what will come of it."

Then the two witches began to scream and protest in a rage, but as soon as they opened their mouths, holy water was dashed into their faces, whereupon they howled more horribly than ever, and at last promised, if their lives were spared in any manner, they would tell the whole truth and disenchant the bride which they did.

Then those present seized the witches and said: "Your lives will indeed be spared, but it is only just that before you go, you will be nicely combed according to the proverb which says: 'Comb me, and I'll comb you!'"

Said and done, but the combing this time drew blood, and the mother and daughter shrank smaller and smaller and then flew away at last as two vile carrion-flies through the window.

And when the story spread around Florence, everyone came to see the house where this had happened, and so it was that the street got the name of the *Via della Mosca* or Fly Lane.

The Dens of the Fairies

THE DENS OF THE fairies are in Fiesole, and are called the Amphitheatre of the Toman Theatre. Behind the Cathedral there is a road going downwards, at the bottom of which is found to the right the remains of the gigantic Etruscan walls. Returning across the open place to the left, we come to the Via delle Cannelle, and in the first farm, also to the left, there is the so-called Roman Theatre. But the people call it Le Buche delle Fate, or Fairies' Dens.

In this farm, where these dens are situated, there was at first an Etruscan settlement. It was said to have been a fortress, and when ruined by wars, its remains were, little by little, covered up, till it all formed a hill. And when this was dug away in modern times, they discovered first of all the remains of walls, and then three arches, and finally, a fountain, called the House of the Fairies. The basin or fountain was then full of fish, and these fish were all people who had been enchanted and changed into that form.

The fairy house was then a splendid palace, and there the fairies kept a public school for boys and girls, and this was called the Scuola delle Signore, or the Ladies' School, and the pupils were so kindly treated that they were happy to go there, and grieved when it was time to go home. The parents were, of course, very pleased by this, and were astonished to find that the pupils were all equal (in proficiency), and that there was not one who was not glad to go to the Ladies' School, for the fairies taught the children different kinds of work, which really delighted them. And, since they learned all this easily and loved the work, the result was that many became distinguished and successful.

Now let us leave for a while the fairies and their work and come to the story.

There was a young lady of noble and wealthy family, who had wedded a *bel signore* of equal condition, and for a time they were deeply devoted.

But as often happened during this time and happens even now, the very greatness and antiquity of his family made the lord more anxious to continue it, and since this did not come to pass, he became cold to his wife, and then finally cruel. Now, this desire to have an heir became in him a single thought, or constant suffering, or lunacy, and since it all turned on his wife, it ended by his wishing her dead so that he might marry another in her place.

The poor lady had always been very pious and good to the poor, and when her husband began to abuse her, she could do nothing but pray and weep, which caused her to turn pale and sorrowful, angering him still more, as if it were another obstacle in the way. Till, finally, one day, after he had returned from the chase and finding her in tears, he had her immediately thrown into a dungeon, ordering that she should receive only bread and water and be treated in a way that would soon cause her death, since he had had enough of such a wife.

Then the lady, reflecting how innocent she was, and how strictly religious and benevolent her life had been, doubted the providence of God, and in despair, called to the Evil One for aid. Nor was the appeal unheard, for it was followed by a distant peal of thunder, and then by louder and nearer crashes, with flashes of lightning and the clanking of chains. All at once, a *diavolo* or evil spirit appeared like a courtly, graceful man, clad in black, but surrounded by light and curling blue flames which played about his head like living hair.

Immediately, the lady in terror repented that she had called him. However, he did not hesitate to address her right away:

> I was summoned by your voice,
> And it made my heart rejoice,
> For I felt that in your air
> Was my own spirit of despair.
> You have called me from afar,
> Even from beyond the farthest star,
> Driven by utter agony,
> What, oh woman, do you want from me?

Then the lady took courage and replied:

> All that I ask of you, put simply
> Is that I may a mother be.

And the spirit replied:

> A lovely maid you soon will bear,
> With mind and heart beyond compare;
> Thus all your suffering and pain,
> Will be made up to you again.
> But I who aid, in consequence,
> Must also have my recompense,
> For when due time shall pass away
> In fifteen years, then, come what may,
> She shall be mine, without delay.

Since the lady was so possessed by the mad desire to have a child and to resume her place in her husband's heart, she assented, seeing no other escape from death or way into a happy life. Indeed, she believed that God had forsaken her, and consequently, nothing could go worse for her.

Then the demon went to her husband, disguised as a wise man, and persuaded him that he had been mistaken as to his wife, for it appeared plainly by the planets that, if she were taken into favor again, she would soon become a mother. As a result, he, whose whole mind was bent on one thing, had her brought from the dungeon, begged her pardon, and she was soon as happy as ever. Nor did the demon fail to keep his word, for, in due time, she became the mother of a maid who grew into a girl of incredible beauty and marvelous mind.

This child, when old enough, was sent to the School of the Ladies, or fairies, who loved her so much that they, knowing all things, began to consider whether something could not be done to save their pupil from the fate which awaited her.

Now, the fairies observed that there was a great waste of straw in the country, and so they invented the art of splitting it into lines and braiding it into kinds of hats and beautiful objects, which art, indeed, first came from Fiesole, where it is still most perfectly practiced. And they taught this art to the little girl. Following their directions, she made a square basket in which to carry her luncheon, and on each side there was a figure of a cross in red and black.

As the fated time of the fifteenth birthday drew near, the mother began to manifest constant anxiety and suffering and did not stop weeping, to the great discomfort of her husband. Then the fairies, who had decided what to do, spoke to the young girl:

> "In a few days, my dear child, your fifteenth birthday will come, and you are destined to experience a terrible danger, and on that day, your mother will try to keep you at home, hoping to have you with her to the very last. But, come what may, despite everything, you must escape and come here to the school. So, now, take this little silver basin, and when your mother weeps, make sure that you gather fifteen of her tears in it. Also, make sure that your mother does not know why you are doing this because, if you do, we cannot help you."

So, on the morning of her fifteenth birthday, the parents of the maid tried to keep her at home. However, she poured the fifteen tears into a vial and took her basket. But, instead of luncheon, she put the vial into it and went on her way. Once she arrived at the school, the strange pale signore was standing there, clad in black. He was under one of the arches awaiting her. But the fairies, upon seeing the maid, threw her into the fountain and told her that, when the demon attempts to seize her, to throw the tears in his face and say:

> For the maiden's fifteen years
> Take her mother's fifteen tears;

For every year, 'tis plain to see,
Is worth a year of agony.

And when she had done and said this, the defeated devil sank in a rage into the ground, spraying and sputtering out sparks like a grand exhibition of fireworks, He did this with such a roar of thunder that it was heard half-way to Rome. So, the girl was free (and all turned out well for everyone for the rest of their days).

And since that time Fiesole has been famous for the straw-work which was first taught by the fairies, as all the old people there know, and to this day, when rabbits are seen running out from the ruins, people say that they are the fairies.

Genzio

THERE LIVED IN FIESOLE a magician named Genzio, who was a man by day and a woman by night, but, as the former, he took delight in roaming through rural scenes, cities, and mountains, floods, and fields, especially where there were horses, which gave him pleasure, as well as cattle of all kinds, and these he depicted with rare skill as an artist. And all the maids of Fiesole adored Genzio, because he had taken their photographs.

And one day, when he was buried in thought in his garden, he was roused from his reverie by a light touch. When he looked up, he saw a very beautiful blonde girl, who evidently was in great distress and begged permission to consult him. But he replied:

> Daughter mine, it may not be
> That you can walk alone with me,
> Nor would your mother deem it fit
> That you with me in the house should sit,
> For I not only am a man,
> But more than that, a magician.
> Girls should of such as I beware,
> Nor fall into a sorcerer's snare.

As he said this, she had in her hand some straw which she was braiding, and as Genzio spoke the last word, the straw turned into a beautiful vase of flowers, which gave forth an exquisite odor, which could be seen from far away. And the maid was amazed, but she soon added:

> Truly, I never dreamed, good sir,
> That you were a conjurer.

Yet, indeed, if one you be,
'Tis the better for me
Therefore, I beg leave to come
For a reason to your home,
And when you've heard what I want to say,
You will not tell me to haste away.

Then she went on to say to him:

As a sorcerer you must know
What evil deeds men do below.
And how the wicked Medici,
Lords of yon city, woe to me!
And lords of all on every side
Abuse their power far and wide—
A power which no law can stem.
Great wrong must I endure from them!

Then Genzio replied that she should return to him in secrecy and by night. And when she came, she was amazed at being received by a beautiful *fata*.[1] But she told her tale, how the Medici had imprisoned her father and threatened to put him to death unless she would surrender herself to their Lod Cosimo, and that this was the last night and limit of the time allowed her.

After having heard this, Genzio replied: "Rest in peace here, and I will provide for everything."

So, she remained, but Genzio went to her *castello* and assumed her very form. Her own mother would have thought he was her daughter, for not a golden hair was missing. And at midnight the guards and ruffians of the Medici came and took her to their master. When she appeared before him, he gazed at her with admiration, which changed into great awe and dread at what he soon beheld. From a maiden of resplendent beauty, she changed to a very tall, stately, and dignified man of commanding presence. He had a very

---

1. Fata is a fairy. [CGL]

heavy long black curling beard, with flowing black robes, and on his head was a circlet of gold, surmounted by a star of dazzling light. In a voice which inspired fear, he said, pointing at the Grand Duke:

> "You evil, corrupt, and thrice-accursed prince! How far will you go in this career to leave behind a name which will be for you and yours as a record of shame forever? You, who should be the father and protector of your servants, have become their scourge and betrayer. Yet, a little more, and the evil days will come upon you, and there will be wailing in your palaces and remorse in your heart, and over all Christendom, you will be called the Vile One. Yet, your punishment may be put off for a few days if you do what I say and free the father of this girl and herself immediately and give them ample recompense for what they have suffered. If this is not done, woe unto you! Your refusal will be your death!"

Then Cosimo di Medici, struck by mortal fear and remorse, did as Genzio had demanded, and the maid was restored to peace and great posterity.

The Unpublished Legends
of Virgil

How Virgil Was Born

And truly this *aurum potabile*, or drinkable gold, is a marvelous thing, for it works wonders to sustain human life, removing all disorders, and 'tis said it will revive the dead.

—Phil. Ulstadt, *Cœlum Philosophorum, seu Liber de Secretis*

And there be magic mirrors in which we may see the forms of our enemies, and the like, battalions for battle, and sieges, and all such things.

—Peter Goldschmid, *The Witch and Wizard's Advocate Overthrown* (1705)

THERE WAS ONCE AN old temple in Rome, in which a very learned Signore by the name of Virgilio, or Virgil, was living. He was a magician, but very good in all things to all men; he had a kind heart and was always a friend to the poor.

Virgil was as brave and fearless as he was good. And he was a famous poet—his songs were sung all over Italy. Some say that he was the son of a fairy (*fata*), and that his father was a king of the magicians. Others maintained that his mother was the most beautiful woman in the whole world, and that her name was Elena (Helen), and his father was a spirit. And how all this came about was as follows:

When all the great lords and princes were all in love with the beautiful Elena, she replied that she would marry no one, having a great dread of bearing children. She would not become a mother. And to avoid further wooing and pursuing, she shut herself up in a tower and believed herself to be safe because it was far outside the walls of Rome. And the door to it was walled up so that no one could enter. But the god Jove entered and did so by changing himself into many small pieces of gilded paper, which came down into the tower like a shower. The beautiful Helen held in her hand a glass of wine, and many of the bits of gold-leaf fell into it.

"How pretty it looks!" Helen said. "It would be a pity to throw it away. The gold does not change the wine. If I drink the gold, I shall enjoy good health and always preserve my beauty."

But hardly had Helen drunk the wine than she felt a strange thrill in all her body, a marvelous rapture, a change of her whole being, followed by complete exhaustion. In time she found herself with child and cursed the moment when she drank the wine. Indeed, this was the way that Virgil, who had a most beautiful golden star on his forehead, was born to her. Three fairies aided at his birth: the Queen of the Fairies cradled him in a cradle made of roses. She made a fire of twigs of laurel; it crackled loudly, and he was born to the crackling of twigs. His mother felt no pain. The three each gave him a blessing. The wind wished him good fortune as it blew through the window. The light of the stars and the lamp and the fire, who are all spirits, gave him glory and song. He was born fair and strong and beautiful. Everyone who saw him was overcome by wonder.

When Virgil turned fourteen, he happened to go to an old solitary temple one day in the summer. The temple was in ruins and deserted, and he lay down to sleep. But before he had closed his eyes, he heard a sound like a voice lamenting, and it said:

"Alas! I am a prisoner!
Will no one set me free?
Most happy he will be."

Then Virgil said: "Tell me who you are and where you are." And the voice answered:

"I am a spirit
Imprisoned in a vase
Under the stone
Which is beneath your head."

Then Virgil lifted the stone and found a vase which was closed. When he opened it, a beautiful spirit appeared and told him that there was also a book of magic and necromancy in the vase.

"In it you will find all secrets
Which you desire to obtain
To make whatever you will into god,
To make the dead speak,
To make them come before you,
To go invisibly wherever you will,
To become a great poet,
You will learn the lost secret
How to become great and beautiful.
You will rediscover the mystery
Of predicting what is to take place
And to win fortune in every game."

Lying by the vase was a magic wand, the most powerful ever known, and from that day on, Virgil, who had been as small as a dwarf, became a tall, stately, very handsome man.

This was his first great work: he made a mirror in which one could see all that was happening in any country in the world, in any city, as well as in any house anywhere. Keeping the mirror hidden (beneath his cloak), he went to the emperor, and because he was a handsome man, well dressed, and also with the assistance of the mirror, he was permitted to enter the hall where the emperor sat. Then, as he conversed with him, the emperor was so pleased that he spoke more familiarly and confidentially than he was wont to do with his best friends. Consequently, the courtiers who were present became angry and jealous.

Turning to Virgil, the emperor said: "I would give a thousand gold crowns to know just what the Turks are doing now, and if they intend to declare war against me."

Virgil replied: "If your highness will go into another room, I can show you in secret what the Turks are doing now."

"But how can you make me see what the Turks are doing? It's more than I can understand," the emperor replied. "However, let us go, if it be only to see what fancy you have in your head."

Then the emperor rose, and after giving his arm to Virgil, they went to a nearby room where the magician showed and explained to him everything that the Turks were planning. And the emperor was amazed at seeing clearly what Virgil had promised to show. Then he gave Virgil a thousand crowns in his own hand and became his friend from that day on. And so, Virgil rose in the world.

The Story of Romolo and Remolo

THERE WAS OF OLD a king who had a beautiful wife, and also two children, twins, who were exactly alike. This king was named Romo and his wife Roma, and the children were called Romolo and Remolo.

Now, it came to pass that the queen and her twins, both as yet sucklings, were besieged in a castle when the king was far away. The enemy had sworn to kill the whole royal family and to eradicate the kingly race. When the queen realized that she was in sore distress and saw death close upon her, a wizard came to her and said, "There is only one way by which you can save your life and that of your babes. I can change you all three into werewolves, and thus in the form of wolves you may escape."

Soon after the queen had the power to become a she-wolf or a human being at her will, and it was the same with the children. So, they fled and lived in the woods for seven years. The boys grew up like young giants, as strong as six common children, and the queen became more beautiful than ever, for she lived under a spell.

One day, when the king was hunting in the forest, he found himself alone and surrounded by such a pack of raging wolves that his life was in great danger. All at once a very beautiful woman appeared, and she seemed to have great power over the beasts, as if she were their queen, for they obeyed her and retreated. Then the king recognized her as his lost wife. So, they returned with the twins to their castle, but the king did not know that his wife and children were werewolves.

At one point, the same enemy who had sought to kill the queen seven years before, about which the king knew nothing, came to the castle pretending to be a friend, and he was kindly treated. But when the queen and her two sons caught sight of him, they flew at him as if they were mad. In fact, they tore him to pieces before the entire court and began to devour him like raging wolves. Yet, the king still did not know the whole truth.

Then the slain king's brother gathered an army and besieged Romo, who found himself in great danger. One evening he said:

> "There is danger within the walls,
> The sound of enemies outside,
> The sun set in blood.
> Tomorrow it may rise to death.
> Would that I had more warriors to fight!
> Two hundred fierce and bold,
> Two hundred would save us all,
> Three hundred would give us full victory."

The queen said nothing, but that night she stole secretly out of the castle with her sons, and when alone, they began to howl, and soon all the werewolves in the country assembled. So, the queen returned with three hundred men, so fierce and wild that they looked like devils.

They were strange in every way, and talked or howled among themselves in a horrible language, which, however, the queen and her sons seemed to understand. And in the first battle Romo gained a great victory, and it was observed that the three hundred men ate the dead. However, the king was glad to have conquered his enemy.

When Romolo and Remolo grew to be men, they learned that, in a land not far away, there were two Princesses named Sabina and Sabinella, who were the two most beautiful, and also the strongest, maidens in the world. And it was also made known that the man who wished to win either maiden had to come and conquer her in a fight and then carry her away by major strength.

So, Romolo and Remolo went to their city, and on a certain day the two princesses appeared in a public place, ready for the combat. Then Romolo advanced with his brother riding on his shoulders, pick-back, as boys do, and, snatching Sabina with one hand and Sabinella with the other, he ran away like the wind, so rapidly that he soon outdistanced all pursuers. And when Romolo was tired, Remolo took his place, carrying the sisters and his brother. And Romolo sang a song about this:

> "Up and down the mountain,
> Over the fields and through the rivulets,
> Over gray rocks and green grass,
> I saw a strange beast run.
> It had three bodies and three heads,
> Six arms and six legs.
> Yet it never ran on more than two.
> Read the riddle rightly, if you can."

The two brothers wished to build a new and great city of their own. So, they went to a certain goddess, who told them:

> "The city which you hope to build will be
> Above all others it will tower sublime,
> And rule the world in a far future time.
> The greatest ever seen in Italy.
> But know that at the first, before it can rise,
> It calls for blood and human sacrifice.
> I know not where the choice or fate does lie,
> But of you two, one must surely die."

Now, everyone had been wishing for a city like this because in those days there were but few in the land. Consequently, the brothers assembled many wolves, bears, foxes, and all wild beasts, and by using their power changed them into men. And here is how they did it: A sorcerer took an ox and enchanted it, and slew it, and sang a magic song over it and left it in an enchanted place. Then the wolves and other wild beasts came by night to the great stone of the sacrifice near a running stream. A god beheld it. They ate the meat—they became men. These were the first Romans.

Last of all a serpent appeared with a gold crown—the Queen of the Serpents. She ate of the meat and became the most beautiful woman in the world. She was a great magician. Thus, she became the goddess of the city and dwelt in the tower of the temple. And her name was Venus. She was like a star.

Then Romolo and Remolo wished to know which of them was to die to save the city. And both desired it. Then they decided to take an immense stone and throw it one at the other. So, Remolo picked it up and threw it at his brother, and all who beheld it thought he must be slain. But Romolo caught it in his hands and threw it back. However, Remolo caught it easily. But in that instant his foot slipped, and he fell backward over the Tarpeian Rock, and so he perished.

This is an old story, and thus it was that Rome was built.

Now, it was in this city, or nearby, that some time later, Virgil was born, who in his day brought about many wonders. But the first wonder of all was the manner of his birth, for Virgil was the glory of Rome, and the greatest poet and sorcerer ever known in Rome.

Virgil and Dorione, or The Magic Vase

MANY CENTURIES AGO IN Naples there was a young man named Dorione, who studied magic, and his master was a great sorcerer named Virgil. One evening Dorione found himself in company with friends, and another wizard named Belsevo was also present. Now, there was not enough bread in the house for supper for all.

"Never mind," remarked Belsevo. "He who has art will find his bread in any part. Observe me."

Taking a large vase, he turned it upside down and said:

> "Come, bread, to me,
> For hungry are we!
> Oh, Ceres, give us bread!
> Grant me this grace benign,
> And I shall ever be true to your kind."

Then he removed the vase, and there were eight small loaves on the table.

Following this display, Belsevo said to Dorione: "Can't you give us wine for the bread, Oh disciple of the grand master Virgil?"

But since Dorione was only a beginner in magic, he could not bring about such a miracle and was much ashamed because everyone laughed at him.

The next morning Dorione told Virgil what had happened.

"You deserved very well to be scoffed at and jeered this way," the master replied. "A young magician should never play tricks at a table like a juggler to amuse fools. But you have been sufficiently punished, and to please you, I shall give you a fine present. And if you cannot make bread appear out of thin air, you will at least have the power to make it and other things disappear. I will give you this bronze vase. It is quite small, as you see, but tell any object, no matter how large it is, to disappear in it, then the vase will swallow it. You are to keep a house for yourself in a secret place, anywhere you wish, and whatever the vase may swallow, you will find it in the house, no matter how far you will be from it. Only say, 'Get into the vase!' and the vase will swallow it up. But you are never to use it to steal, or for any dishonest purpose. So long as you are honest, it will serve you, and nobody will rob you of it. And if that should happen, call to it, and it will return to you."

Then Dorione took the vase and thanked the grand master Virgil. After some time passed, the young scholar went on a long journey. Dorione possessed a small castle in a remote place in the mountains of Tuscany, and in it was a secret vault. "Here is where I will send everything that the vase may swallow," he said. Many a thing may be obtained honestly, if one knew how to send it away and where to put it.

> "He who has a cage, I've heard,
> In time will surely get a bird."

Soon thereafter he became the secretary of a certain lord, who, like many of the brave gentry of his time, was continually at war with somebody, plundering or being plundered, each one in his turn, as fortune favored.

> Up on the top of the hill today,
> Down in the dale tomorrow,
> Often in the morning happy and gay,
> After a night of sorrow;
> For some must fall so others may rise
> And the swallow goes chirping as she flies.

One evening Dorione's master heard a trumpet in the distance, and, as he looked outside, he seemed suddenly startled, like a man in great alarm. Pointing to a splendid suit of armor, he said, "Do you see that armor, Dorione? It is worth ten thousand crowns, and I would give ten thousand if it were in hell this instant. I took it in a raid from the Grand Duke, and he will be here in ten minutes with all his men. If he finds the armor, I shall lose my head. And there, too, is an iron chest full of gold and jewels—all plunder, and all in evidence against me."

"If you will give it to me," Dorione answered, "I will make it all vanish in an instant."

"Indeed! I give it to you with all my heart, but be quick about it, for the Grand Duke and his soldiers are at the gate, and I feel the rope round my neck!"

Then, within a minute, Dorione brought his vase and uttered the conjuration:

> "Begone! begone!
> All you fine things which are now my own,
> Fly to my castle—never stop!
> Beautiful vase, now open your jaws."

And in an instant the armor and chest went flying into the vase and disappeared. Just as they vanished the Duke and his men entered. Though they sought in every cranny, they found nothing. Consequently, having come for a bargain of wool, they went away shorn, as the proverb says.

"You have saved my life," said the signore. "God only knows how you made the things disappear, but you are welcome to them. Truly, I was glad to get them, but a thousand times better pleased to see them go."

One day the signore and Dorione found themselves in a battle together, sorely beset and separated from all their troops. They were in most extreme danger of being killed, when all at once Dorione, who had his vase slung to his side like a canteen, had an idea. He pronounced the spell, ordering all the arms in the hands of the enemy to fly through the vase to his castle. In an instant swords and spears, daggers and battle-axes, left their owners, who stood unarmed and amazed. Consequently, the two were saved.

The signore took a great deal of booty and rewarded Dorione very liberally, the more so because he was greatly delighted to see the gifts disappear into the vase. No matter what, all was fish to that net, and all the sheep black—and Dorione liked to please his kind master, especially in this way. Yes, to amuse him he would often wish away a gold-hilted and jeweled sword or helm from an enemy and was pleased to hear the brave old knight laugh to see the things fly.

The signore's generosity stopped, however, at a certain point. He had a beautiful daughter whom Dorione loved, to distraction, but the father would not consent to bestow her on him. However, one day the castle was besieged by a vast force, which spared neither man, woman, nor child, and it seemed plain that the besieged would have to yield. Then the lord asked Dorione to make the enemy's weapons vanish.

"This time," replied his secretary, "I cannot do it. The fame of my vase and my power has spread far and wide, and the enemy have had their weapons enchanted by a mighty sorcerer, so that I cannot take them."

So, they fought on until only Dorione, the lord, and his daughter were left alive in the garrison. They were in extreme danger of being killed.

"And now," thought Dorione, "something must be done, for there are many wolves at the door. Let me see if I can make the young lady go into my vase, and then her father."

So, he brought them together and said:

> "Lovely lady, lady my own,
> The fairest whom earth has ever known,
> Fly in a hurry, oh, fly away!
> Leave the castle—flee while you may,
> And off to my distant shelter flee!
> The beautiful vase will make you free.
> It will open its mouth to take you in.
> And you will be safe when once within!"

In a second, before the eye could follow, the young lady was whirled away mysteriously, and, then her father after Dorione uttered the spell. Then the young man prayed to the spirit of the vase, who was no other than Saint Virgil himself, to save himself as well. And in an instant, he felt himself swallowed up like a bean in the mouth of a horse. Within seconds he found himself in the vault of the castle with the lady and her father, who were amazed to see what wealth had been gathered there. Indeed, Dorione had been very industrious in the many battles he had fought and had sent weapons and booty to his home.

Then all three joined hands, danced and sang for joy to find themselves safe. Dorione and the lady did the most rejoicing because the signore had promptly said:

"After this you may get married."

And they had the wedding that night. As a proof of the affection and esteem the signore felt for Dorione, he gave a speech of regret as a penance for not having sooner consented to the nuptials, ending with these words: "And now let everyone here present drink a cask of wine, and get roaring drunk as four fiddlers."

Giovanni of Bologna and the God Mercury

MANY YEARS AGO IN Florence, the Tuscans worshipped the idols of Jupiter, Bacchus, Venus, and Mercury in their temples. And sometimes those gods, when evoked, came down to earth. In those days there was in Florence a sculptor from Bologna named Giovanni, the same who made the imp in the Old Market. He was tormented by the desire to make a statue of such beauty that would be unique in the entire world. Moreover, he desired that this statue should appear to be alive, one not stiff and fixed, but one like Mercury, always active. He was so full of this thought that he had no rest even at night, for a certain gentleman had said to him: "You are intoxicating yourself all in vain by studying statues and declaring this one is beautiful, that even more so, or this sculptor has talent, and that one even cleverer. Yet, after all, the best of their work is motionless and seem to me to be corpses. For me a real clever sculptor would be one who could make a statue inspired with motion like a living man who runs and hops, not a sculptor who merely carves a statue out of a piece of marble."

And these words from the gentleman moved Giovanni to make a statue which would be unique in the world. Consequently, he thought of Mercury, the liveliest and quickest of all the gods, who is always flying like a falcon. And he said to himself:

> "If I could behold him,
> Though it were but for one time,
> I would have the model
> Of a wondrous statue
> Inspired unto life!"

One evening Giovanni found himself in the Temple of Mercury, which is called today the Baptistery of Saint John, and there he found Virgilio, to whom he said that he greatly longed to see Mercury living and in flight. Then Virgilio replied:

"Go at midnight to the hill of Vallombrosa when the moon is full and call the fairy Bellaria, who will help you."

Giovanni went to the hill and called to Bellaria, but she made no reply. So, he returned to Virgilio, who said: "It is not enough to simply call to her, she must be conjured by an incantation."

Then Giovanni learned the incantation and conjured her:

> "Shining star!
> Resplendent glowing air,
> With your burning splendor,
> Bell' Aria, inflame,
> Inspire great Mercury,
> Make him descend to earth
> That he may copied be.
> You who are beautiful,
> As beautiful as good,
> Grant me, I pray, this grace,
> For I am lost in grief
> Because I cannot make
> A statue as I wish.
> Behold, Bellaria!
> I've come up this hill
> To beg this thing of you!
> I pray you'll grant my prayer,
> For I am unhappy."

Evoked by Mercury's plea, Bellaria responded thus:

> "Mercury, beauteous God!
> By the rushing water!

By the glowing heaven!
As you shine, reflecting again
Their beauty, and as the wind
Or the lightning you are fleet.
I too like you are fleet,
Conjured and compelled
Even by my own splendor
To inspire, inflame
You by my own heat!
So that you will descend to earth,
So that Giovanni, born
In Bologna, may
As sculptor copy you!
I pray you to descend,
Just like lightning's flash.
Until you are measured,
I shall not have peace
Being myself invoked.
If you will grant this grace,
Yet not for me but Giovanni,
Please give me three signs:
The flash, the crash and bolt.
If you will grant me this grace,
Please give me three signs."

Then, within seconds, there was a flash, roar, and thunderbolt,
and Giovanni from Bologna beheld Mercury flying in the heaven, and
said:

"You are too little and light, by far!
I cannot paint a shining star,
Nor the wind or the lightning!
All hope is lost, ah me! Amen!"

Then the beautiful Bellaria said: "If you cannot depict Mercury flying through the air, it may be that you can paint him flying over the waves, for then his speed is not so great."

So she invoked Mercury again, as he was seen flitting over the ocean. But when Giovanni from Bologna beheld Mercury leaping from wave to wave like a dolphin, he cried out:

> "Farewell, fair Mercury, all is over.
> I'm but a mortal and no more,
> Can I depict your face again,
> And least of all your wondrous grace."

In response, Bellaria said to him: "You have asked too much. It is not possible for you to make fire and water come to life. Yet, be at ease, for what may not be done in water or in air may come to pass with ease upon the earth."

Bellaria again invoked Mercury, who descended like the wind in a leap, who leaps down on earth. Then Giovanni cried:

> "Thanks to God!
> Now I have the idea!"

And so, Giovanni made the beautiful statue of Mercury in bronze, and so long as the Tuscans worshipped their idols, they were accustomed to dance, but after they stopped this worship, they danced no more.

The Girl and the Flageolet

"Thus playing sweetly on the flageolet,
He charmed them all, and playing yet again,
Led them away, won by the magic sound."

—De Pueris Hamleensibus, 1400

THERE IS IN THE region of Toscana Romagna a place known as The Valley of Hunger, in which a family of peasants, or three brothers and two sisters, were living. The elder brother had married a wife, who was good and beautiful, and she had given birth to a daughter, but died when the babe was only one year old. Then, according to the advice of the sisters and brothers, he married again so that he might have someone to take care of his child. The second wife was a pretty young woman, but after she had been wedded a year, she gave birth to a daughter, who was very ugly, indeed, and evil, but the mother seemed to love her all the more for this and began to hate the elder stepdaughter who was as good and beautiful as an angel. As the stepmother's hatred grew, she beat and abused the poor little girl all day long.

One morning the girl went into the woods to hide herself from her stepmother until evening, when she could return home and be safe with her father and aunt. And while sitting all alone beneath a tree, she heard a bird above her singing so sweetly that she was enchanted. It was a marvelous sound, at times like the music of a flute played by a fairy, then like a human voice caroling in soft tones, and then like a horn echoing far away. The little girl said: "Oh dear, sweet bird, I wish I could pipe and play like you!"

As she said this, the bird fell from the tree, and when she picked it up, she found that it was a *zufolo*, or a shepherd's flageolet, in the form of a bird. Then, as she blew it, it gave forth such sweet sounds that anyone who heard them would be charmed. She began to practice playing it and discovered that the art of playing it seemed to come of itself. Moreover, every now and then she could hear a fairy voice in the sound speaking to her. Now, this was a miracle created by Virgil the magician, who did so many wonderful things in olden days.

In the evening she returned home and played on the bird-pipe, and everyone was charmed except the stepmother, who was the only one to hear in the music a voice which said:

> "Though sweet your smile, and smooth your brow,
> Evil and cold at heart you are.
> I never yet did harm to you;
> Yet you have beat me cruelly,
> And given me curses fierce and wild
> Because I'm fairer than your child.
> Unless you now leave me alone,
> All ill will be your own
> With all the suffering I have known."

But to the girl the pipe sang:

> "Sing to your father, gently say
> That you the morrow will go away,
> And tell him you have borne too long
> Great cruelty and cruel wrong;
> For truly he was much to blame
> That he so long allowed the same.
> But now the evil spell is broken.
> The time has come, the word is spoken!"

Then her father would have gladly kept her, but she was spellbound and went out into the wide world playing on her pipe. When she was in the woods, the birds and wild beasts came and listened to her and did as she wished. When she was in towns, the people gathered around her and were charmed to hear her play. They gave her money and often jewels, and no one dared to say an evil word to her, for a spell was on her, and a charm kept away evil.

So, years passed by, and she was blooming into maidenhood, when one day a young lord, who happened to pass by with his mother, a woman as noble of soul and good as her son, paused to hear the girl play on her pipe and sing, for they thought the marvelous song of the *zufolo* was her voice.

Then the lady asked the girl if she would enter a monastery, where she would be educated and brought up to live in a noble family in return for her music. The girl replied that she had already a great deal of money and many jewels, but that she would be very glad to be better educated to advance in life. So, she entered the convent, where she was very happy. The result was that she became betrothed to the young signore, and great preparations were made for the wedding.

Now, the stepmother had but one idea in life, which was for her own daughter to make some great match. Consequently, she was glad when the stepdaughter had departed, and she hoped she would become a mere vagabond, playing the flute for a living. But when she heard that the girl had become very prosperous in a convent in Florence and had not only been educated like a princess in the best society, but would also marry a nobleman, she became mad with rage. So, she went to a witch and paid her a great sum to prepare a powder which, if strewed in the path of the bride, would cause her to feel prompt and agonizing pain, and after a time, death in the most dreadful suffering. The powder was to be spread on the path of the wedding procession. But on that morning the pipe sang:

> "Wherever on earth the wind does blow,
> All leaves and dust before it go.
> Evil or good, they fly away
> Before its breath, as if in play.
> And so shall it for you this day,
> Ashes to ashes and dust to dust,
> And death to the witch, for so it must
> Forever happen as it was decreed,
> For death is the pay for an evil deed!"

Now, the bridegroom and all friends had begged the bride to play the flute as she walked in the wedding procession. When she did so, it seemed to her that it had never played so sweetly. The stepmother was looking on anxiously in the crowd, and when the bride was just coming to the powder on the path, the wicked woman cried: "Play louder—louder!"

So, to oblige everyone, the bride blew hard, and a wind came from the pipe which blew all the powder into the stepmother's eyes and open mouth, and in an instant, she uttered a cry of agony, and then rolled on the ground, screaming, "The powder! I have swallowed the powder!" And the flute played:

> "By your mother I was slain.
> A fairy gave me life again.
> I was killed for jealousy,
> And all as false as false could be.
> Now you are dead and I am free."

And from that time onward, the pipe played no more. But the young lady married the signore, and all went well with them. And all this was caused by Virgil, who was as benevolent as always.

Virgil and the Girl with Golden Locks

And they had fixed the wedding day,
The morning that must wed them both,
For Stephen to another maid
Had sworn another oath;
And with this other maid to church
Unthinking Stephen went.
Poor Martha, on that woeful day,
A pang of pitiless dismay
Into her soul was sent.

—Wordsworth, *Poems of the Imagination: The Thorn*

THERE WAS ONCE IN Florence a wealthy widow, a lady of noble family, who had a son, who was all that a parent could have wished, had he not been somewhat reckless, dissipated, and also selfish. He showed all this by winning the love of girls and then leaving them. His behavior became such a scandal that it caused great grief to his mother, who was a truly good woman. So, once the young man, who was really a devoted son, realized this, he reformed his ways for a long time.

But as the proverb says, he who has once drunk at this fountain will always remember the taste, and probably drink again. Consequently, as time passed, the young gentleman fell again into temptation and began to tempt and corrupt, albeit with greater care and caution. Indeed, all timid sinners generally act this way. They resolve the next step will be the last until finally, under solemn promise of marriage, he led astray a very poor and friendless maiden into the very forest of despair. She was exquisitely beautiful and known as "the girl with golden locks" because of her hair. The young man might have kept his word, but at an evil time he was tempted by the charms of a young lady of greater wealth and greater family, who met him more than halfway, giving him to understand that her hand was to be had for asking. As a result, he, who never lost a chance or left a fruit unplucked, asked at once and was accepted. Then the wedding day was set at once.

In the meantime, when the girl with the golden hair found herself abandoned, she became virtually desperate. Before long, she gave birth to a child, which was a boy. And it was some months after this, indeed, before the wedding of the young man to the heiress was to take place, that one day, as the young unmarried mother was walking along the Arno, she met the great poet and sorcerer Virgil, who saw in her face the signs of such deep suffering, and of such a refined and noble nature, that he paused and asked her if she had any cause for her affliction. So, with little trouble he induced her to confide in him, and she revealed that she had no hope because her betrayer would soon be wedded to another.

"Perhaps not," replied Virgil. "Many a tree destined to be chopped down has escaped the axe and lived until God blew it down. On the appointed day, we three will all go to the wedding."

And truly, when the time came, all the people of Florence were very much amazed to see the great Virgil entering the Church of Santa Maria with the beautiful girl with the golden hair bearing her babe in his arms. So, the building was quickly filled with people eagerly waiting to witness some strange sight.

And they were not disappointed. For when the bride in all her beauty and the bridegroom in all his glory came to the altar and paused before the priest spoke, Virgil stepped forward, presented the girl with golden locks, and declared: "This is the young maiden you are to wed since you swore to make her your wife, and this is your child."

Then the infant, who had never before in his life uttered a word, exclaimed in loud, sweet tones:

"You are my father, I'm your son.
Other father I have none."

Then there was a great scene. The bride was extremely mad, and everyone cried out, "Hurrah, Virgilio! If the Signore Cosino does not wed the girl with golden hair, he will not escape us!"

Of course, he did, indeed, marry her, and that not so unwillingly, for the sight of the girl and the authority of Virgil, the cries of the people, his own conscience, and the marvelous occurrence of the babe's speaking reconciled him to it.

So, the wedding was carried out right away, and every soul in Florence who could make music went with his instrument that night and serenaded the newly married pair. Indeed, Signor Cosino's mother was quite astonished when she saw her son, who had gone forth with one bride, return with another. However, she was soon persuaded by Virgil that it was all for the best, and found in time that she had a perfect daughter-in-law.

The Magician Virgil;
A Legend from the Sabine

THERE ONCE WAS A wizard, who lived with his wife (who was a witch) and their beautiful daughter in a house with a fine garden full of broccoli—Oh! the finest broccoli in the world![1] Across from this house and overlooking this garden, two women dwelled, and one of these was pregnant.

"Cousin," she said to the other woman, "how I'd like to have two broccolis from the magician's garden. They're so nice!"

"Yes, cousin, but how can we get them? It would be dangerous!"

"It can be done at midnight when the sorcerer is asleep if we steal just a little."

So, at midnight they each went with a sack, climbed over the iron gate, filled their bags, and went away.

In the morning the magician Virgilio went to his garden and found that many broccoli were missing. In a rage he ran to his wife, and said: "What's to be done?"

She replied: "This night we'll set the cat on guard upon the gate."

They did that, and in the evening at sunset, one of the women said:

"Ah, cousin, this night it can't be done."

"And why not, my dear?"

"Why? Because they've set a guard."

---

1. The following tale was obtained by Miss Roma Lister from the vicinity of Rome, and from an old woman who is learned in sorcery and incantations. It begins with the note that, on February 8, 1897, it was taken down as given, literally word for word, and I translate it accordingly verbatim. The influence of the classical tale "Rapunzel" is clear. [CGL]

"Guard! An old cat, you mean. Are you afraid of her?"

"Yes, because she meows when she sees something."

"I'll tell you what we'll do. We'll take a bit of meat, and when she opens her mouth to meow, we'll throw it inside. That'll keep her jaws quiet while we pick the broccoli."

Said and done, and they got away with another bagful of broccoli.

In the morning the magician Virgil found that he had been robbed again.

And again, he complained to his wife, who said: "Well, tonight we will put the dog on guard."

Said and done. But the dame at the window was on the watch. And when she saw the dog, she said:

"No broccoli tonight, cousin. This time they've put the dog to keep a lookout."

"Oh, forget the dog! When he opens his jaws to bark, I'll throw in a good bit of hard cheese. That'll keep him quiet."

Said and done again. The next morning the magician found that even more broccoli had disappeared from his garden.

"The thing is becoming serious," he said. "Tonight I'll watch myself."

After saying that, he went to his gate and remained there, looking closely at all those who passed by, and when the first man walked by, he asked, "What is your trade?"

"I'm a carpenter."

"Move on," replied the magician. "You're not the man I want."

Then another came.

"What's your calling?"

"I'm a tailor."

"Move on. You won't do."

Then a baker came. He was not wanted. But the next was a sexton and digger of ditches and graves, and the wizard cried: "Bravo! You're my man! Come with me; I want you to dig a pit in my garden."

So, the poor man went, for he was just as much frightened by the terrible face and stature of the wizard as he had hope in being paid. Once he was directed to a specific place, he dug a hole nearly as deep as the magician was tall.

"Now," said the master, "get some light sticks and cover the pit with them while I stand in it, and then spread some twigs and leaves over it with a few leaves to hide the top of my head."

Once it was done, and Virgil stood there totally covered, the sexton hurried away, glad that he had dug this strange grave for another, and not for himself.

Evening came, and one of the cousins looked out the window.

"Good! There's not even a dog on guard. Come, let's hurry! This time we will take all that remains of the broccoli."

Said and done. And when they had gathered the last plant, one of the cousins cried: "Look! What beautiful mushrooms! Let's pick them."

She had seen the two ears of the sorcerer, which peeped out uncovered. So, she took hold of one and pulled.

"It won't come out!" she cried. "You pull one, while I draw this mushroom."

Each pulled until the magician lifted his awful face and glared at them.

"Now you will die for robbing me!" he exclaimed.

They were in a fine fright. At last, Virgil said: "I shall spare your life," he said to the pregnant woman, "if you give me all that you are carrying—everything within you."

She consented, and they departed. After some time had passed, she became a mother, and the magician came and demanded the child. And since she had promised it, she consented to give the baby to him, but begged him to allow her to keep the infant for a while.

"I shall let you have the babe for seven years," he replied.

After saying this, he left her in peace for a long time. So, the child, who was a boy, came into the world, and as he grew older, he was sent every day to school.

One morning the magician met him and said: "Tell your mother to remember her promise."

Then he gave the child some sweets and left him. When he returned home, the boy said: "Mamma, a gentleman met me today at the door of the school and said that I should tell you to remember your promise. Then he gave me some comfits."

The poor mother was in a great fright and responded: "Tell him, when you next meet him, that you forgot to give his message to me."

The next day the boy met the magician and said to him that he had forgotten all about it and had told his mother nothing.

"Very well, tell her this evening and be sure to remember."

The mother heard this and told him to tell the sorcerer the same thing again.

When the boy met the magician Virgil again and told the same story, the latter smiled and said: "It seems that you have a bad memory. This time I'll give you something by which to remember me. Give me your hand."

The boy gave his hand. Then the magician bit into one finger, and when the child screamed, Virgil said: "This time you will remember."

The boy ran yelling home.

"See what has happened to me, nasty mamma! All because I did what you asked and told the gentleman that I forgot."

The poor woman, hearing herself called nasty mamma, was overcome with grief and shame, and said, "All right. I'll tell him myself."

So, the next day she took the child and gave him to the magician, who led him to his home. But when his wife, the witch, beheld the boy, she cried:

"Kill that child at once, for I read it in his face that he will be the ruin of our daughter Marietta!"

But the magician declared that nothing would induce him to harm the boy. So, the little fellow remained and was treated by the master like a son. In due time he became a tall and handsome young man, and he was called Antonuccio. But the witch continued to say: "We should kill and eat him, for he will be the ruin of our Marietta."

At last, the magician became weary of her complaints and said, "Very well. I'll set him a task. And if he cannot accomplish it, I'll slay him that very same night."

Now, since Antonuccio slept in the next room, he had overheard all this. Then the next morning the magician took the young man to a stable which was very large and horribly filthy, the likes of which no one had ever seen.

"Antonuccio," the magician said, "you must clean this stable completely, repave the ground, and whitewash it from top to bottom. Moreover, when I speak, an echo will answer me."

The poor youth soon went to work but soon found that he could do next to nothing. So, he sat down in despair.

At noon Marietta came to bring him his lunch and found him in tears.

"What's the matter, Antonuccio?"

"If you knew that I am to be killed this evening—"

"What for?"

"Your father has said that unless I clean out the stable, and pave and whitewash it to the echo—"

"Is that all? Cheer up! I'll take care of all this."

Marietta went home and entered on tip-toe while the sorcerer slept. Then she quietly carried off his magic wand, and with a few words, she cleaned out the stable to the echo, and Antonuccio was delighted.

In the evening the magician came, and when he found the stable clean as a new pin, he was very pleased and kissed him and took him home. The witch-wife was furious at learning that the stable had been cleaned. She declared that Marietta had done it and ended by screaming for his life. At last the wizard said: "Tomorrow I shall set him another task, and if he should he fail, he will surely die."

The next morning he led the young man into a dense forest of mighty trees and said: "You see this forest. In one day, you must cut down all the trees and clear them away so that you can make a clean field, in which all kinds of plants in the world can grow there."

So, Antonuccio began to hew with an axe and worked well, but he soon gave up the task in despair. At noon came Marietta with her basket.

"What, crying again! What is the trouble today?"

"Only to clear away this entire forest, make a clean field, and plant it with all the herbs in the world."

"Oh, well, eat your lunch, and I'll see about it. Lucky for you that it's not something difficult!"

She ran home, got a magic wand, and went to work. Down the trees came crashing—away they flew! It was a fine sight, upon my word! And then up sprouted all kinds of herbs and flowers until there was the finest garden in the world.

The magician returned in the evening and was very pleased to see how well Antonuccio had done the work. But when his wife heard about it, she raged more than ever, declaring that it had all been done by Marietta, who was destined to be ruined by the boy.

"Very well!" exclaimed the wizard. "Since you are not giving me any peace, I must put an end to this trouble. I'll give the boy nothing to do tomorrow—he may remain idle—and in the evening I will chop off his head with this axe."

Antonuccio heard them talking just as he had done on the other occasions, and this time he was in despair. In the morning Marietta found him weeping.

"What's the matter, Antonuccio?"

"I don't have to do any work today, but this evening I am to have my head chopped off."

"Is that all? Cheer up! I'll see what can be done."

She put the pot on the fire to boil and began to make the macaroni. When she had cooked a great deal, they fed all the furniture, pots and pans, chairs and tables, to please them and induce them to be silent—all except the hearth-brush whom they forgot by oversight.

"And now," said Marietta, "we must be off and away. It's time for us to go!"

So away they ran. After a while the wizard and his wife returned and knocked at the door. No answer. They rapped and called, but got not reply. At last, the hearth-brush cried:

"Who's there?"

"Marietta, open the door—It's me."

"I'm not Marietta. She has run away with Antonuccio. First, they fed everybody with macaroni, but they gave me none."

Then the witch cried to the wizard: "Hurry—quick—catch them if you can!"

The good man did as he was told and began to travel—far and fast.

All at once, while the lovers were on their way, Antonuccio turned his head and saw that their pursuer was on a mountain road and cried: "Marietta, I see your father coming."

"Then, my dear, I will become a fair church and you will be the fine sexton. He will ask you if you have seen a girl and young man pass by, and you will reply that he must first repeat the Paternoster and not the Ave Maria. If he asks again, tell him to say the Ave Maria and not the Paternoster. And then, he will lose his patience and will depart."

This was how the wizard was deceived. After he returned, his wife asked him what he had seen.

"Nothing but a church and a sacristan."

"Stupid that you are! The church was Marietta—fly, fly and catch them!"

So, he set forth again, and again he was seen from afar by Antonuccio.

"Marietta, I see your father coming."

"Good. Now I will become a beautiful garden, and you the gardener. And when my father comes and asks if you have seen a couple pass by, reply that you are weeding lettuces, not broccoli. And when he asks again, answer that you are weeding broccoli, not lettuces."

This is how everything happened, and the wizard lost his patience and returned home.

"Well, and what did you see?" his wife inquired.

"Only a garden and a gardener."

"How stupid can you be? Those were the two. Let's start! This time I will go with you!"

After a while Antonuccio saw the two following them and gaining on them rapidly.

"Marietta, here come your father and mother. Now we are in a nice mess."

"Don't be afraid. Now I will become a fountain, fair and broad, like a small lake, and you a pretty pigeon. They will call you, but for mercy's sake, don't let yourself be taken in, otherwise it will all be over for us."

The wizard and his wife came to the fountain and saw the dove. They tried to inveigle and catch it with grain. But they couldn't catch it, nor could the witch quench her thirst with the water. So, when she realized that both were beyond her power, she cried and cursed in a rage: "As soon as Antonuccio kisses his mother, he'll forget Marietta and every other."

Then, when the parents departed, the pair set forth again, until they came to a place not far from where Antonuccio's mother was living.

"I will go and see my mother," he said.

"Don't go, for she will kiss you, and you will forget me," replied Marietta.

"But I will take good care that she doesn't kiss me," Antonuccio answered. "Just wait a day."

So, he went to see his mother. Both were in great joy at meeting again, but he implored her not to kiss him. Then, since he was weary, he went to sleep, and his mother did not heed his request and kissed him while he slept. When he awoke, Marietta was completely forgotten.

So, the witch's curse worked, and he lived with his mother. Soon he fell in love with another girl. Then they appointed a day for their wedding.

Meanwhile, Marietta lived where she had been left and made friends with a fairy, who knew about everything that was happening far and near. One day she told Marietta that Antonuccio was to be married.

Marietta begged her to go and steal some dough from the house of the bride. The friend did so, and Marietta made two cakes in the form of puppets from the dough, or children, and one she called Antonuccio and the other Marietta.

Then on the day of the feast, the first day of the wedding, she begged her friend to go and put the two puppets on the bridal table.

The fairy did so, and when all the people were assembled, the puppet Marietta began to speak:

> "Do you remember, Antonuccio,
> How, when my father brought you to his house,
> My mother wished to take away your life?
> And how he asked you to sweep the stable clean?"

And the other replied:

"Passing away, passing away,
Well do I remember the day."

Then Marietta sang:

"Do you remember, Antonuccio,
How I helped you to clear the field?"

He replied:

"Passing away, passing away,
Well do I remember the day."

She sang again:

"Do you remember how you hadn't worked
Upon the day when they wanted to murder you,
And how we fled together to escape?"

He replied:

"Passing away, passing away,
Well do I remember the day."

Meanwhile the true Antonuccio, who was present at the table, began to remember what had taken place. Then the puppet Marietta began to sing again:

"Do you remember how I was the church
And how you became the sacristan?"

He answered:

"Passing away, passing away,
Well do I remember the day."

"Do you remember how I was a garden,
And how you became the gardener?"
"Passing away, passing away,
Well do I now remember the day."
"Do you remember how I was a fountain,
And you a pigeon flying over it?"
"Passing away, passing away,
Well do I now remember the day."
"Do you remember, Antonuccio,
How my mother laid a curse on me,
And, how she said before she went away—
'When Antonuccio kisses his mother
He'll forget Marietta and every other?'"
"Passing away, passing away,
Well do I now remember the day."

Then Antonuccio himself remembered everything, and rising from the table, he ran from the house to where Marietta was living and married her.

Virgil, Minuzzolo, and the Siren

VIRGIL HAD A PUPIL named Minuzzolo, who was very small indeed, but a very handsome youth, and the great master was fond of his disciple. Since Virgil wished that little Minuzzolo should learn about all the wonders hidden in the earth, he said to him one day:

"I want you to know, Minuzzolo, that we are going on a long journey which may last for years, and you will have to be right brave, my boy, for many are the perils through which we must pass, and dire are the monsters which we shall meet."

So, they went forth into the world, far and wide, and little Minuzzolo showed himself as brave as the biggest, and as eager to learn as a whole school with a holiday before it when students shall have learned their lessons. And here are the things he learned: how to resist all sorceries and evil spells; he could call the eagle down from the sky, and the fish from the sea; but there was one thing he did not learn from his master.

One day Virgil gave him a book, which contained the charm against the Song of the Siren, the words which protect those who know them against the music of the Voice. However, two pages stuck together like one, so that Minuzzolo skipped two pages, and never knew the charm. Virgil had gone out, and Minuzzolo, seated in a hut in the forest where they lived, began to sing. Then he heard a girl's voice in the woods that seemed to come from a torrent, singing in answer. It was so sweet that all his soul and senses were captivated. He forgot all duty and desire, his master and everything, all in a mad yearning to follow the sound. Consequently, he went on and on, led by the song. He didn't notice whether it was day or night. The voice went with the torrent. He followed it to a river, and the river to the sea, where the waves rolled high in foam and fog. He followed the song. It went deep into the sea, but he gave no heed and kept on going.

Then he found himself in a very beautiful but extremely strange old city—a city like a dream of an ancient age. And as evening approached, the young man asked this and that person where he might spend the night, and they all said they didn't know of any place because strangers never came to that city. However, at last someone said to him, "I know where a witch lives, and she often has strange guests. Perhaps she will give you shelter."

"I'll go to her," replied Minuzzolo.

"Better not," was the reply. "I was only joking, and I'd be sorry if so fair a young man like you were to be devoured by some monster."

"I have very little fear of that," replied the young magician. "Whoever has never harmed anyone, need not fear anyone, and in the name of my Master I am safe."

Consequently, he went to the house and knocked, and an old woman of unearthly ugliness came to the door. Minuzzolo saw at once that she was a sorceress. So, when she asked what he wanted, he replied:

"In the name of him whom all
Like you obey, and heed his call,
And tremble at his slightest word,
Virgil, my master and your lord,
I beg you to give me food and rest,
Whatever you can and only the best!"

And she answered:

"Whatever is asked in that dread name,
I'm sworn to answer to the same."

So, the young man stayed there and was well served. In the morning he thanked the old woman and asked her where he could find Virgil. Then she replied: "Don't search for him in the forest where you left him. Since then you have passed over half the world. It was a Siren, who called you, and nobody can resist her unless they learn the spell. Your master anticipated that you would be in danger, and this is why he gave the spell to you. However, you didn't learn it. And now I'll give you a ring which will be of use to you, but don't seek its help until you are in dire need. Then you are to say to it:

'In the name of the great magician!
In the name of Virgil!
To whom be all good,
This ring will be my spouse!'"

"I shall remember it well," replied Minuzzolo.

So, he went on and crossed the land and walked along the strand until he came to a great and fine ship. When he stopped to look at it, he thought he would like to be a sailor. Therefore, he asked the captain if a boy was needed. And the captain, who was pleased by his looks, took him and treated him very kindly. So, for three years Minuzzolo was a sailor.

But one night there was a great storm, and suddenly, a tremendous wave and gale of wind came that blew Minuzzolo into the sea, and he floated a mile before he was missed. However, he managed to get to a beach and scramble ashore, where he lay for a long time as if asleep. Yet, it seemed to him, while he was thinking of the captain and his mates that he was being carried away on and on as if in a dream. Indeed, when he awoke, he found himself in what he knew had to be another country, in another climate. He was very hungry, and once he saw a fine garden in which delicious fruit was growing, he approached a tree to pluck a pear. All at once, however, a terrifying man with eyes like a dragon sprang and threatened him with death. In response, Minuzzolo drew the ring from his pocket and repeated the charm, and as he did this, the sorcerer fell down dead. Then he heard the voice of the Siren singing from a distance. The sound of the voice drew nearer and nearer until a beautiful girl appeared. When she saw the hideous sorcerer lying dead, she exclaimed with joy: "At last I am free! The great master Virgilio has done this! He has used his power over land and sea. Blessed be his name!"

Then she explained to Minuzzolo that she and others had been enslaved and enchanted, and then compelled to become sirens and to bewitch men. But Virgilio had known that she was lurking near to charm his pupil. This is why he had given him the book to read. But the evil sorcerer had used his power to close the pages so that Minuzzolo had yielded to her song. Finally, Virgilio summoned a greater power, and used it so that the Siren herself became enchanted with love causing the sorcerer to be defeated. Soon Virgilio appeared and blessed the young couple, who were then married and lived happily ever after.

Such were Virgilio's deeds.[1]

---

1. This strange story, in which classic traditions are blended with the common form of a fairy-tale, was sent to me from Siena, where it had been taken down from some authority to me unknown. [CGL]

Virgil and the Peasant
of Arezzo

Dress if you will
A knave in silk, he will be shabby still.

IN OLDEN DAYS, PEOPLE suffered many things far more than they do now, firstly from the signori, who treated them worse than brutes, and as if this were not enough, they were tormented by witches and wizards and wicked people, who went to the devil or his angels to revenge them on their enemies.[1] However, there were good and wise men, who had the power to conquer these evil ones, and who did all they could to untie their knots and turn back their spells and curses on themselves, and the greatest of these was named Virgilio, who passed all his life in doing good.

Now, it is an old custom in Arezzo that, when men take cattle to a fair, be it oxen or cows or calves, the animals are dressed out or ornamented as much as possible, and there is great competition with regard to this among the peasants, for it is a great triumph for a peasant when all the people say that his beasts made the finest show of any in the place. Consequently, it is said that a man of Arezzo will spend more to bedeck his cattle for a fair than he will to dress his daughters for a dance.

Well, there was a very worthy, honest man named Gianni, who was the head or manager under the proprietor of a very fine estate near Arezzo, and one day he went to the fair to buy a yoke of oxen. And what he cared for was

---

1. This legend, with several others, was gathered in or near Arezzo.

to get the best, for his master was rich and generous, and did not much heed the price so that he really got his money's worth.

But good as Gianni was, he had to suffer the affliction which none can escape of being envied and hated, for wicked and spiteful souls find something to hate in people who have not done them any wrong, and whom they have not the least motive to harm.

Consequently, the good Gianni found at the fair a pair of oxen, which, so far as ornament was concerned, were a sight to behold. Indeed, they were covered with nets and adorned with many bands of red woolen stuff all embroidered with gold, and bearing in gold the name of their owner, having many cords and tassels and scarfs of all colors on their heads. And, these cords were elaborately braided, while there hung a mirror on the forehead of each animal so that the elegance of their decoration was the admiration of all who were at the fair.

As Gianni watched the oxen draw near, he waited before making an offer. First, he complimented the owner on their beautiful appearance, and when this was done, he said: "All very fine, but in doing business for my patron I set aside all personal friendship. Your cattle are finely dressed up, but how are the beasts themselves? That is all that I care to know, and I don't wish to have them turn out as it happened to a man who married a wife because he admired her clothes, and found, when she was undressed that she was a mere scrap and looked like a dried cod-fish."

So, they talked until the dealer took off the coverings, and Gianni found, in fact, that the oxen had many faults.

"I am sorry to say, my friend," Gianni remarked, "that I cannot buy them. I have done you more than one good turn before now, as you well know, but business is business, and I am buying for my master, so good-day."

Then the owner was in a great rage, grated his teeth, and swore revenge, for there were many people about who laughed at him, and he resolved to do evil to Gianni, who, however, thought no more of it, but went about the fair until he found a pair of excellent oxen which were the best for sale. Then he drove them home.

But as soon as the oxen were in the stable, they fell to the ground dead. Gianni was in despair, but the master had seen the cattle and had found them fine and in good condition when they arrived. So, he did not blame him.

The next day Gianni went to another fair, and bought another yoke of oxen. But when in the evening they were in the stable, they fell dead at once, just as the others had done. Still the master had such faith in Gianni, that although he was greatly vexed at the loss, he told the man to go to a fair once more and try his luck. So, Gianni went, and indeed returned with a magnificent pair of oxen, which were carefully examined, but there was the same result, for they also fell dead, soon as they were stabled.

Then the master decided to go and buy cattle for himself, and did so. However, the result was the same: these oxen fell dead like the others. And the master, in despair and rage, said to Gianni: "Here I'm giving you some money, and now be gone, because I believe that you're bringing evil to me. I have lost four yoke of oxen and don't want to lose any more."

So, Gianni went forth with his wife and children in great suffering. In his place the master hired Dorione, who was the very man who had owned the oxen which Gianni would not buy, and he was one who was versed in all the sorcery of cattle, as such people in the mountains always are, and he had used his witchcraft to bring about everything that had happened.

Now, under his care, all the cattle flourished wonderfully, and the master was very pleased with him. But Gianni was in extreme misery and could see nothing but the life of beggary before him, because word spread everywhere that he brought bad luck, and he could no longer get any employment.

One day, when matters were at their worst with him, and there was not even a piece of bread in his poor home, he met a troop of cavaliers on the road. At the head of this group were two magnificently clad gentlemen, the Emperor and Virgil.

The poor peasant had stepped aside to admire the procession as it passed, when all at once Virgil looked with a piercing glance at Gianni and cried: "Man, what is causing you to suffer so much? You seem so wretched. Your face is revealing that you are suffering unjustly almost to death."

Then Gianni told his story, and Virgil answered: "For all of this there is a remedy.

"Now come with me to the house of your late master, where there is work to be done."

"But they will drive me out head first," replied Gianni. "I don't dare to go there. And if I do not return to my family, who are all ill or starving to death, they'll think that something disastrous has happened to me."

"For that, too, there is also a remedy," said Virgil with a smile. "Have no care. Let's be off to your master!"

Once they arrived at the farm, Virgil asked the padrone, "Why did you send this honest man away?"

Immediately, the master replied by telling Virgil all about the oxen.

"Since he brought ruin into my house, I had to dismiss him," he said.

"Well," replied Virgil, "this time you got rid of an honest man and kept the knave. Now let us go and see what's wrong with your dead oxen."

So, they went to the place where the dead oxen had all been thrown, and where the whole eight lay unchanged, for they had not decayed yet, and they were as sound as ever.

Then Virgil exclaimed, as he waved his wand:

> "If you are charmed, retake your breath
> If you're bewitched, then wake from death!
> Speak with a voice, and tell us why
> And who it was that made you die!"

Then all the oxen came to life and sang in chorus with human voices:

> "Dorione slew us for revenge,
> Because Gianni would not buy his oxen.
> Truly they were greatly ornamented,
> Yet all were wretched, sorry cattle.
> All this caused Dorione to swear revenge,
> And he did this by bewitching us."

"You have heard the whole truth," said Virgil to the Emperor. "It is for you to condemn the culprit."

"I condemn him to be put to death at once," replied the Emperor. "Have you anything to add?"

"Yes," said Virgil. "I condemn him to become a goat immediately after death."

Then Dorione was burnt alive because he was such an evil wizard, and he leapt from the flame in the form of a black goat and vanished.

Gianni returned in favor to his master, and all went well with him ever after.

Virgil and the Bronze Horse

But evermore their moste wonder was
About this horse, since it was of brass.
It was of faerie as the peple seemed,
Diverse folk diversely han deemed.

—Chaucer, "The Squire's Tale"

ONE DAY VIRGILIO WENT to visit the Emperor, and not finding him in his usual good temper, he asked what the matter was, adding that he hoped it would be in his power to do something to relieve him. Then the Emperor complained that what troubled him was that all his horses seemed to be ill or bewitched, behaving like wild beasts, or as if evil spirits were in them. What grieved him most was that his favorite white horse was most afflicted of all.

"Do not vex yourself about such a thing," replied Virgil. "I will cure your horses and all the others in the city." Then he brought about the making of a beautiful horse of bronze, and it was so well made that no one, unless through Virgil's will, could have made the like. And whenever a horse suffered in any way, and he beheld it, the animal would be cured at once.

All the smiths and horse doctors in Rome were greatly angered by this because, after Virgil made the bronze horse, they had nothing to do. So, they planned to take revenge on him, and they all assembled in a vile place frequented by thieves and assassins, and there they agreed to kill Virgil. But when they went to his house at night to search for him, he had escaped. So, upon finding the bronze horse, they broke it into pieces and then fled.

When Virgil returned and found the horse in fragments, he was greatly grieved and said: "The smiths have done this. However, I will yet do some good with the metal, for I will make a bell out of it, and when the smiths hear it ring, I will give them a peal to remember me by."

Consequently, the bell was made and given to the Church of San Martino. The first time it was tolled, it sang:

> I was a horse of bronze, and tall.
> My enemies broke me to pieces small.
> But a friend who loves me well
> Had me made into a bell.
> Now here on high I proudly ring,
> And as I *ding! dong!* sing,
> I tell aloud, as I toll and wave,
> Who is a cuckold and who a knave.

When all the smiths who had broken the horse heard the bell, they became as deaf as posts. Then great shame and remorse came over them, and they threw themselves down on the ground before Virgil and begged his pardon. Then Virgil replied: "I pardon you, but, for a penance, you must have six other bells made to add to this one. Then you must put them all in the same church where they will make the same peal together."

This they did, and then regained their hearing.

Virgil's Magic Loom

I heard a loom at work, and thus it spoke,
As though its clatter like a meter woke,
And echoed in my mind like an old song,
Rising while growing dimmer just like smoke.
And thus it spoke, "God is a loom like me,
His chiefest weaving is Humanity,
And man and woman are the warp and woof,
Which make a mingling light of mystery."

—Charles Godfrey Leland, *The Loom*

GEGA WAS A GIRL fifteen years old, and without parents or friends, with nothing in the world but eyes to weep and arms to work. Yet, she was fortunate since an old woman, a fellow-lodger in the place where she was dwelling, was moved by compassion and took the girl to live with her, though all she had was a very small room with a poor bed and a little loom, so crazy-looking and old that it seemed impossible to work with it.

Nunzia, for such was the old woman's name, took Gega indeed as a daughter, and taught her to weave, which was a good trade in those days, and in that place where few practiced it. So, it came to pass that they made money which was put aside. Indeed, this was no great wonder, for the old loom was strangely enchanted and could produce marvelous work.

The old woman very often instructed Gega to take great care of the loom, and the girl could not understand why Nunzia thought so much of it, since it seemed to her to be like any other. In fact, it never appeared strange to her that when she wove, the cloth seemed almost to produce itself, and that its quality or kind improved as she applied herself to work, for in her ignorance she believed that this was the way with all weaving.

At last, old Mamma Nunzia died, and Gega, left alone, began to make acquaintances and friends with other girls who came to visit her. Among these was one named Ermelinda, who was at heart as treacherous and rapacious as she was shrewd. Moreover, she knew just how to flatter with perfection and with her beauty and deceitful airs so that she could make a simple girl like Gega believe that the moon was a pewter plate, or a black fly, white.

Now, the first time that she and several others, who were all weavers, saw Gega at work, they were greatly amazed, for the cloth seemed to produce itself from a wretched old loom which appeared to be incapable of making anything, and it was so fine and even, and had such a gloss that it looked like silk.

"How wonderful! One would say it was silk!" cried a girl.

"Oh, I can make silk when I try," answered Gega.

And, applying her will to it, she soon spun a yard of what was certainly real silk stuff from cotton thread. Upon seeing this, everyone present declared that Gega must be a witch.

"Nonsense," she replied. "You could all do it if you tried as I do. As for being a witch, it is Ermelinda and not I who should be so, for she first said it was like silk, and made it so."

Then Ermelinda saw that there was magic in the loom and that Gega knew nothing about it. Therefore, she decided to do everything in her power to obtain it. And this she achieved at first by flattery, and gave the innocent girl extravagant ideas about her beauty, assuring her that she had an attractiveness which could not fail to win a noble husband, and that, since she had put aside a large sum of money, she should live on it in style until married, and that in any case she could go back to her weaving. Ermelinda laid most stress on getting Gega to leave her old lodging and getting rid of her dirty old furniture, especially the horrible, crazy old loom. Indeed, she persuaded her that, if she ever should have occasion to weave again, she, with her talent, could do far better with a new loom, and probably gain thrice as much, all of which the simple girl believed, and so let her false friend dispose of everything. Then when Ermelinda did this, she did not fail to keep the loom herself, declaring that nobody would buy it.

"Now," Ermelinda said, "I am content. You are very beautiful. All that you need is to be elegantly dressed, and have fine things about you so that you can soon catch a fine husband."

Gega agreed to all this, but was loath to part with her old loom, which she had promised Nunzia should never be neglected. Yet, Ermelinda promised so faithfully to keep it carefully for her that she was persuaded to let her have it. Then the young girl took a fine apartment, well-furnished, and bought herself beautiful clothes. Guided by her false friend, she began to go to social gatherings and make fashionable friends, and live as if she were rich.

Then Ermelinda, after having obtained the old loom, went to work with it, in full hope that she too could spin silk out of cotton, but found out to her amazement and rage that she could do nothing of the kind. In fact, she could not so much as weave common cloth from it. All that she got after hours of fruitless effort was a headache, and the conviction that she had thrown away all her time and trouble which made her hate Gega all the more.

Meanwhile Gega enjoyed life for a time as she had never done before. But, though she looked anxiously to the right and the left for a husband, she found none. The well-to-do young men, quite as anxious to wed wealth as she was, discovered on inquiry that she had little or nothing, despite her style of living, and her money rapidly melted away, until at last she found that to live she had to work—there was no help for it. So, with what remained of her money, she bought a fine loom and thread and sat down to weave. Though she succeeded in making common stuff like others, it was not silk, nor anything like it, nor was there anyone who would buy what she made. In despair, she remembered what Mamma Nunzia had solemnly said to her, that she must never part from the old loom. So, she went to Ermelinda to reclaim it. But her false friend, although she could do nothing with the loom herself, was not willing that Gega, whom she hated with all her heart, should in any way profit. So, she declared that her mother had broken it and burned the rubbishy old thing. When Gega insisted on having proof of it, Ermelinda adhered to this story and drove her in a rage out of the house.

In the days when Mamma Nunzia was alive and wise, she had carefully taught Gega the properties and nature of plants, roots, herbs, and flowers, saying that someday it might be of value to her, as it is to everyone. So, whenever they had a holiday, they had gone into the fields and woods, where the girl became so expert that she could have taught many a doctor very strange secrets. Moreover, Nunzia had also made her learn the charms and incantations which increase the power of the plants. So now, having come to her last coin, and finding there was some profit in it, she began to gather herbs for medicine, which she sold to chemists and others in the towns. Then, when she found a deserted old tower in a wild and rocky place, she was allowed to make it her home. Indeed, after all she had gone through—her disappointment in friends and lovers—she found herself far happier when alone than when in a town, where she was ashamed to meet people who had known her when she lived in style.

One evening as she was returning home, she heard a groaning in the woods as if someone was in great suffering. Guided by the sound, she found a poor old woman seated on a stone, who told her that she had hurt her leg by slipping from a rock. So, Gega, who was as strong as she was kind and compassionate, carried the poor soul in her arms to the tower, where she applied some healing herbs to the wound and told her that she was welcome to remain.

"I have nothing to give you for all that you have done," said the old woman on the following day.

"But I did not do it in the hope of anything," replied Gega.

"And yet," said the sufferer, "I might be of use to you. If, for example, you have lost anything, I can tell you how to recover it or where it is."

"Ah!" cried Gega. "If you can do that, you will be a friend indeed, for I have lost my fortune. It was a loom, which was left to me by Mamma Nunzia. I did not regard her advice never to part with it, and I have bitterly repented my folly. I trusted it to a friend, who betrayed me, for she burned it."

"No, my dear, she did nothing of the kind," replied the old woman. "She still has it, and I will make it return to you."

Then she repeated this invocation:

> "Loom! Loom! Oh loom!
> Who by the labor and skill

Of the great magician Virgil
Were made so long ago,
And gifted with such power,
I ask you, by that skill
And labor given by
Virgil, the great magician,
As you can spin a web
Of silver or of gold,
Fly like the wind away
From Ermelinda's house
Into the small old room
Where once my daughter dwelled,
All by the skill and power
Of great Virgilius!"

All at once they were borne away on a mighty wind and found themselves in the old room, and there they also found the loom. Now Gega could weave cloth of gold or silver as well as silk at her will. Then the old woman looked steadily at Gega, and the girl saw the features of the old woman change to those of Nunzia, and as she embraced her, the old woman said:

"Yes, I am Mamma Nunzia, and I have come from afar to restore your loom to you. But guard it well now, for if lost, you cannot recover it again. But if you should ever need anything, then invoke the grand magician Virgil because he has always been my god."

After saying this, she departed, and Gega knew now that Nunzia was a white witch or a fairy. So, Gega became rich again and was a lady, and ever after this episode in her life, she took good care of her loom and distrusted flattering friends.

Virgil, the Wicked Princess, and the Iron Man

An iron man who did on her attend,
His name was Talus, made of yron mould,
Immoveable, resistlesse—without end.

—Spenser, *Faerie Queene*

THERE ONCE LIVED A princess, who was beautiful beyond words, but wicked beyond belief. Her entire soul was given to murder and licentiousness. Yet, she was so crafty as to escape all suspicion, and this pleased her best of all, for deceit was to her as dear as life itself. All this she managed, as many another did in those days, by inveigling through her agents handsome young men into her palace by night, where they were invited to a banquet and then to a bed, and all went gaily till the next morning at breakfast, when the princess gave her victim in wine or food a terrible and rapid poison, after which the corpse was carried away secretly by her servants to be thrown into the river, or hidden in some secret vault. Thus, it was that the lady sinned in secret while she kept up a decent name before the world.

Now it came to pass that a young man, who was a great friend of Virgil, was taken in the snare by this princess and put to death. Thereafter, he was no longer heard of, but when the great poet used his magic art, he learned the whole truth. Consequently, for revenge or punishment, he made a man of iron with golden locks, very beautiful to behold as a man with a sympathetic, pleasing air, one who conversed fluently and in a winning voice. Yet, he was made entirely of iron, and the spirit, who was conjured into him, was one without pity or mercy.

Then Virgil made the Iron Man walk back and forth in front of the palace of the princess. Once she saw him, she was more pleased than she had ever been before, and she immediately sent out a messenger, who invited him to enter the palace by a secret gate, which he did. Then he was warmly received and treated with a great display of love. In the morning, at breakfast, the princess hesitated to give him the deadly drink, for she had at last fallen madly in love. Then, suddenly, he said: "Well, where is the poison? Don't keep me waiting! Quick, let me drink it!"

When the princess heard this, she was indeed terrified, thinking, "This man knows all about my secret." But as she hesitated, he took the deadly cup and drained it to the last drop.

"And now," she thought, "I am saved."

But the Iron Man said with scorn, "Do you call *that* stuff poison? Why, it would hardly kill a mouse. Give me stronger, I say, stronger poison! I live on poison, and the stronger it is the better I like it."

Hearing this, the princess felt herself from head to foot as if her blood had been turned all to ice, for now she knew that she was lost and her punishment at hand.

"And now," said the Iron Man, "since all the poisoning and treachery and putting to death of young gentlemen is at an end, you must come with me!"

Upon saying all this, he took her under his left arm and went forth.

As soon as they heard her screams, all her retainers came armed, and after them twenty soldiers, but they were all of no avail against such an enemy, whom they could neither pierce with steel nor restrain by force.

Escaping with her, the Iron Man mounted a black steed, which a Moor was holding outside, and with his victim, he flew over the land till they came to a dark and savage place in the mountains. And here he carried her into a vast cavern, where many men were seated around a table, and as she looked, she saw that they were all the lovers whom she had put to death. Then they all cried: "*Ecco la nostra moglie!* Behold our wife! Behold out Drusiana!"

And another said: "Let us give her something to drink, and let us drink to her!"

So, they gave her a full goblet, which she could not help swallowing, and the wine was like fire, the fire of hell itself in all her veins. The men, who had gathered there, burst into laughter at seeing her suffering, and one of them shouted:

Drink, princess, drink!
You feel the same fire,
Only in greater measure,
Hotter, wilder and fiercer,
Which you did feel before,
When your blood boiled with passion,
And with love of secret murder.
Then you did feel it a little.
Now you shall feel it greatly.
Once it ran drop by drop,
Now in full goblets and frequent.

Then another man gave her a glass of wine which she could not help swallowing. And it was cold, and her blood again grew cold as ice, and she shivered in an agony of freezing. And so, it went on, everyone giving her first the scalding hot wine and then the cold, while everyone sang in chorus:

We give you again in your heart
What you did give to us.
The heat of love which burned in us,
Burned in us and in you.
And the cold of desire when satisfied,
You had no mercy on us,
And so we have little for you.[1]

---

1. The connection of Virgil with the classic Talus, or Iron Man, and so many other ancient legends, as shown in these which I have gathered, renders the more striking the assertion that "after the sixteenth century the Vergilian legends disappear and become known only to scholars," as worded by E. F. M. Beneche in his translation of Domenico Comparetti's work. The truth is, that as the age of credulity and mere marvels passed away among the higher classes, the learned ceased to collect or take an interest in heaping up "wonders upon wonders." But the people went on telling and making tales about Virgil, just as they had always done. [CGL]

Virgilio as a Physician, or Virgil and the Mouse

Now to signify destruction and death, they paint a *mouse*. For it gnaweth all things, and works ruin.

—Hori Apolli, *Hieroglyphica* (Rome, 1606)

THERE ONCE LIVED IN Florence a young gentleman—*un gran signore*—who wedded a beautiful young lady to whom he was passionately attached, as she indeed was for a time to him. But "fickle and fair is nothing rare," and it came to pass that, before long, she gave her love again to an intimate friend of her husband. And the latter did not indeed perceive the cause, but he was much grieved at the indifference in him which his wife began to show.

Then the wife began to tell her lover how her husband had scolded her for her neglect, and how much afraid she was lest their intrigue would be discovered, and that she was so uneasy that she was ready to poison her spouse "if she could only get rid of him!"

Her lover replied that there were many ways to get rid of a man without really killing him, for a violent death would lead to suspicion, inquiry, scandal, and perhaps legal punishment. And then he hinted that a better method would be to consult a witch.

The lady lost no time in running to one, to whom she told her whole story, and what she wanted, and since she began by paying a large fee, the sorceress promised she would have her wish. Then the witch prepared a flask of water and powder with magic skill. The water she gave to the wife and told her to sprinkle it over her husband's clothes. Then she changed herself into a mouse, and after she was carried to the bedroom which the married couple occupied, she gnawed a hole in the mattress. Once she crawled inside, she dragged the bag after her and so remained hidden.

When the husband went to bed, there came over him an utter weakness and sickness so that he lay in pain as if dead, and this grew worse day by day. In vain, his parents called in the best physicians, and every remedy was tried to cure him without result.

Then Virgilio, who knew much and suspected all the rest of this affair, was angry that so vile a woman and her gallant should inflict such torture on an excellent and innocent man. So, he decided to intervene in the affair.

Soon afterward, he dressed himself as a *medico*, or doctor, from some distant land, saying that he had heard of this extraordinary case of illness and would like to see the sufferer. To which the parents replied that he was welcome to do so since all the professors of medicine in Florence could make nothing of it.

The doctor looked steadily for some time at the patient, who appeared to be in such utter prostration and misery that he might have moved the hardest heart. By him sat his wife, pretending to weep, but counting to herself with pleasure the time which would pass before her husband should die—giving now and then a suspicious glance at the newcomer.

Then Virgilio said to the wife: "Signora, I beg you to leave the room for a while. I must be alone with this man!"

Whereupon she, with a great show of tears and passion, declared she would not leave the room because her husband might die at any minute, and she would never be able to forgive herself if she were to be absent and so on. To which Virgilio angrily replied, that she might depart in peace with the assurance that her husband would be cured. So, she went out, cursing him in her heart, if there was a chance that he might be able to do what he declared.

Then Virgilio took a mirror which he had brought with him, and placing it before the eyes of the invalid, told him to look at it as steadily and as long as he could. The young man did so, and then said, as if in despair: "For me there is no remedy, Oh doctor, for what you show me is worse than my disorder, as I supposed it to be. Truly, I see death, and not myself."

"Courage!" replied Virgilio. "You shall be cured."

"Cure me," he answered, "and you shall have all that I possess."

"Nay, I shall cure you first," said Virgilio, "and then settle on easier terms."

The patient looked steadily at the mirror. Virgilio rapped three times with a wand when there suddenly leaped from the bed a mouse, which uttered three horrible piercing screams. The doctor told the invalid to continue to look steadily at himself in the mirror, and if he valued his life not to cease doing so. Without turning around, the doctor ordered the mouse to enter the bed and lick up and bring away with her tongue all the water which the wife had sprinkled on the clothes. When this was done, he told her to carry away all the powder which she had placed on the bed. Once this was done, he ordered the mouse to make a pellet from the powder and devour it. But here she resisted, for to do so meant death to her and a cure to the invalid.

However, the doctor was inflexible, and she had to obey. Then no sooner had she begun to eat it than he told the husband to rise which he did, feeling perfectly recovered though much confused at such a sudden change.

Then Virgilio ordered the mouse to mount the bed, and lo! She changed to a woman, for she was, of course, the witch who had done all this devil's work. And the sorceress told them to call the parents, the wife, and everyone. And when they came, the witch said:

> "Evil my life has been, and evil will be the death which in a few
> minutes will come to me. Yet, I am not as evil as this woman,
> who would have killed her husband who loved her by making
> him suffer a horrible death. Hell has many who are bad, but the
> worse are they who return evil for good. And he who has ended
> this thing by his power is the great Virgilio, who is the lord of
> magic in this land."

Then she told, step by step, how the wife had turned her heart from her husband, almost as soon as she was married, and wished to kill him and had paid her to bewitch him. After this, Virgilio opened the window, and the witch indeed died, or it was the last anyone saw of her, for with a horrible howl she vanished in the night, flying away.

The husband recovered and would have given Virgilio all his wealth, but he would accept nothing but the young man's friendship. And the guilty wife was imprisoned for life in a castle, far away in the mountains and alone.[2]

---

2. Virgil appears as a *physician* so distinctly in this and other tales as to induce the question whether he had not, quite apart from his reputation as a poet and magician, some fame as professor of the healing art. [CGL]

Romani Tales

A True Story

Flint and Steel, or How the Sun Was Created

"Tell me another story about the creation."

I was not there at the time, but I heard a great deal about it from my grandfather. All he did there was to turn the wheel. People tell me that the world was made from the sun, but gypsies, who do everything all the contrary, say that the sun was made from the earth. A bad horse is one which will not travel either way on a road.

Once in olden days, just as now, there was a great old witch, who made enchantments and lived all alone in the sky in the night. One day she found a flint in a field, and picked it up, and the stone told her that her name was "Flint." After a bit of time, the witch found a small piece of steel, picked it up, and asked his name, and he replied, "Steel." So, she put the two in her pocket and said to Flint, "You must marry Master Steel." Therefore, they did, but one day the two began to quarrel, and Steel gave his wife Flint a severe blow in the eye that made sparks fly and set fire to the old woman's pocket. Consequently, she threw the burning pocket up into the sky and told it to stay there until a man and his wife who had never quarreled came there. The sparks from Flint's eye are the stars, and the fire is the sun, and it has not gone out as yet and will burn on many a year, for all I know to the contrary.

"Is all this true?"

I was not there.

The Gentleman and the Gypsy

ONCE A GREAT GENTLEMAN would not let a poor, poor, poor Gypsy stay on his farm. So, the Gypsy went to a field on the other side of the way, opposite the gentleman's residence. That night the gentleman's house fell down. Not a stick of it remained standing, only the people who lodged there escaped with their lives. And the gentleman's little babe would have died if a Gypsy woman had not taken it into their poor little tent.

Believe me, that's all *true as my father*, and to this day they call that field the Gypsy Field.

The Gypsies and the Smugglers: A True Story

ONCE, ALMOST A HUNDRED years now, when my father was a boy, numerous Gypsies were walking together near the sea one night, when all at once the horses began whinnying and kicking and neighing. In short, they made a great deal of noise. Then the Gypsies heard a scream and saw men running from a cave and rushing as if in alarm. When they had all departed, the Gypsies went there and found many little barrels of brandy and valuables, for those men were smugglers, and the Gypsies took all they left behind. Indeed, that was a great thing for the Gypsies, and they drank like horses, and the girls and women walked about in silk clothes for many days.

All this happened near Bo-Peep, a great field in the hills close to Hastings in Sussex.

When smugglers lose and Gypsies find, nobody is the worse for it.

The Gypsy and His Three Sweethearts

ONCE A YOUNG MAN courted three girls together, and none of the three knew he was courting the other two. The young man lived in a little place near the side of the great salt water, and one night all the girls came at once together to him, and none of the girls knew the others were coming there. So, they went quickly all together to him and said, "Good evening," at the same time.

Well, the young man did not know which girl liked him best, or whom he loved best. Consequently, all the four of them sat down together at the table, and he gave them food and beer. One ate plenty, but the other two would eat nothing. One drank, but the other two would not drink anything because they were all angry, grieved, and worried. Then the young man told them he was afraid, if he took a wife who could not eat, she would not live. So, he married the girl who ate her food.

Always eat all the food that people share with you, and you will readily endure sorrow and trouble.

The Gypsy and the Snake

IF YOU KILL THE first snake you see, you'll kill the principal enemy you have. That is what they say, but I don't know whether it is true or not.

Well, once there was a very bad man who was always doing bad deeds. One day he saw a snake in the forest and ran after it with a large knife in his hand and cut her head off. Then he said to himself, "Now that I've killed the snake, I'll take the life of my most vindictive enemy." Well, just as he spoke that word, he struck his foot against the roots of a tree, fell down, and drove the knife into his own body.

As he lay dying in the forest, he said to himself, "Yes, I see now that it is true what they told me as to killing a snake, for I never had any worse enemy than I have been to myself, and what comes of killing innocent animals is naught good."

The Gypsy and the Bull

ONCE THERE WAS A Gypsy, who was a great fighting man, a strong man, a great boxer, very bold and fierce. He said many a time that no man and nothing on the roads could frighten him. But one day, as he was walking along the road with his friend, exaggerating and bragging and boasting, and praising himself and swearing that he could beat the old devil himself, they heard a bull bellowing and growling, and the first thing they knew, the bull ran like mad at them. So, the men hurried and climbed a tree, and the great fighting man, who was so handy with his fists, was the first to climb and placed himself furthest from the ground on the limbs of the tree. Meanwhile, he sat there and saw the bull tossing and throwing the Gypsy's baskets all about, dancing on his things, and breaking all his possessions to pieces. Moreover, whenever the wind blew, he was afraid he would fall on the horns of the bull. As a result, the Gypsy and his friend sat there until daybreak when the man, who looked after the cows, came walking by and saw these fellows sitting like birds on the tree. Consequently, he asked them why they were doing that. Well, they told him about the bull, and the man drove the bull away. They came down and went on to the tavern. Indeed, never were there two men in this country who wanted a drop of beer more than they. After that day, the thirsty Gypsy never boasted that nothing could ever frighten him.

Very true, indeed.

The Girl and Her Lover

ONCE, MANY YEARS AGO, a girl was going to steal an egg.

"Let me be," said the egg, "and I will show you where you can get a duck."

So, the girl got the duck, and it said to her, "Let me go, and I will show you where you can get a goose."

Then she stole the goose, and it cried out, "Let me go, and I'll show you where you can steal a turkey."

And when she took the turkey, it said, "Let me go, and I'll show you where you can get a calf."

So, she got the calf, and it bawled and wept and cried, "Let me go, and I'll show you where to find a fine horse."

And when she stole the horse, it said to her, "Let me go, and I'll carry you to a handsome, rich gentleman, who wants a sweetheart."

So, she got the nice young gentleman and lived with him pleasantly one week. But then he told her to go away. He did not want her anymore.

"What a bad man you are," wept the girl, "to send me away! For your sake I gave away an egg, a duck, a goose, a turkey, a calf, and a fine horse."

"Is that true?" asked the young man.

"By my dead father!" swore the girl. "I gave them all up for you, one after the other, and now you send me away!"

"So help me God!" said the gentleman. "If you lost so many things for me, I'll marry you."

So they were married.

Yes, there are false truths and true lies. You may kiss the book on *that*.

Gypsy Truth

MASTER, DO YOU WANT me to tell you the entire truth,—yes? If it's a big or a little thing.

I'll tell the truth, so help me God, upon my life! The devil be in my soul if I tell the least lie! And what is it? Did I ever in all my life steal a chicken? And what do the gypsies do with the feathers, because nobody ever saw any near a gypsy tent? Never, sir,—I *never* stole a chicken. What's more, in all the sixty years that I've been on the roads, in all that time, I never saw or heard or knew of a gypsy stealing one. What's that you say?—Petulengro told you yesterday that he had carried a gun to kill *chickens*! Ah, yes, sir,—that is true, too. The man meant in his heart pheasants. But not *domestic* chickens. Gypsies never steal *them*.[1]

---

1. There is a great moral difference, not only in the gypsy mind, but in that of the peasant, between stealing and poaching. But in fact, as regards the appropriation of poultry of any kind, a young English gypsy has neither more nor less scruple than other poor people of his class. [CGL]

The Man Who Lived
on the Moon

"TELL ME ANOTHER STORY about the moon."

Yes, my dear. In olden days, many men lived happily on the moon with nothing to do but keep up the fire, which makes everything glisten with light. But among the folk lived a very wicked, obstinate man, who troubled and hated all the other nice people, and he managed to drive them away from the moon. And when the mass of the folk were gone, he said, "Now those stupid dogs have gone, and I will live comfortably and well, all alone."

But after a bit of time passed, the fire began to diminish, and this man found that, if he did not want to be in the darkness and die of cold, he had to go and look for wood all the time. When the other people had been there, they never did any carrying or splitting wood in the daytime, while now he had to take it all on his shoulders all day and night. So, the people here on our earth see that man to this day, all burdened with wood, and bitter and grumbling to himself, and huddling alone by his fire. In the meantime, the poor people, whom he had driven away, went all across and around heaven, here and there, and set up business for themselves, and they are the stars and planets and lesser lights, which you see all about.

Merlin and Trinali

"MY UNCLE, TELL ME a pretty story!"

Yes, my child. I will tell you two, and perhaps three, if you keep very quiet. Listen to me. Once in Wales, there was a great wizard named Merlin, and he could do many magic things. He knew how to change one living being into another, iron into silver, and silver into gold. A fine thing that would be if I could do all this. Well, afar from him lived a great witch, whose name was Trinali. Indeed, a great witch was Trinali! Many men did she enchant, many gentlemen did she change into asses and pigs, and never cared a copper for all their sufferings.

Now, one day, Merlin took his magic rod and went afar to find the witch and punish her severely for all her wickedness. But on that very day the lady Trinali heard how Merlin was a great, powerful wizard, and said, "What sort of a man is this? I will punish him, or he will kill me. May the spirits help me bewitch him! We'll see who is more clever and who knows the most."

In the meantime, Merlin went on the road all day alone, always in sunshine, and Trinali went into the forest, always in the shade, the darkness, the gloom, for she was a black witch. Soon they found one another, but Merlin did not know she was Trinali, and Trinali did not know that the man was Merlin. And he pleased her very much, and she, him. Very soon the two began to love one another very much. When one knows that, and the other knows it, both will soon know it. Merlin and Trinali said, "I love you" at the same time and kissed one another, and sat down wrapped in the same cloak, and conversed happily.

Then Merlin told her he was going to punish a very wicked witch, and Trinali told him the same thing, how she was bold enough to do the same thing to a great wizard. And the two began to beg one another to let the thing go, and she and he were afraid of losing lover and sweetheart. But

Merlin said, "I swore by the sun to change her for her entire life into another shape," and she wept and said, "I swore by the moon to change that wizard into another person just as you did."

Then Merlin inquired, "What is his name?"

She said, "Merlin."

He replied, "That's me. What is your name?"

She cried aloud, "Trinali."

Now, when witches swear anything on the sun or the moon, they must do it or die. Then Merlin said, "Do you know how to make this business all nice and right?"

"Not at all, my dear love," said the poor witch, as she wept.

"Then I am cleverer than you," said Merlin. "An easy and nice thing it is, my bride. For I will change you into me, and myself into you. And when we are married, we two will be one."

Well, today, some people say that she conquered him, and another that he conquered her. I don't know which it was, my dear. Did you ever see a two-headed halfpenny? Yes? Throw it up, and when it falls down, ask me which side is under. A Welsh man told me that story. Welshers always tell the truth.

The Gypsy, the Pig, and the Mustard

ONCE A GYPSY WENT to a great farmhouse while the gentleman sat at table eating. As soon as the Gypsy looked away, the gentleman very quietly filled a cheese cake with mustard and gave it to the Gypsy. When the mustard hit his throat, he was half choked, and the tears came into his eyes.

The gentleman asked him, "What are you weeping for now?"

And the Gypsy replied, "The mustard took my breath away."

"I hope the mustard will give you good luck!"

"Thank you, sir," answered the Gypsy. "I'll take care that it does."

As soon as the gentleman turned his head, the Gypsy stole the mustard pot with the silver spoon, and no one saw it. The next day after that incident, the Gypsy went to the gentleman's pig pen and saw a great fine-looking pig there.

"I'll see if I can make you weep a bit," the Gypsy said.

Now, sir, you must know that, if you give a pig mustard in an apple, he can't cry out or squeal for his life, and you can carry him away, or throw him onto a wagon and get away, and nobody will know it. And that is what the Gypsy did to the pig with the same mustard that he had tasted. As the Gypsy put the pig into a bag and ran away with it, he whispered softly into the pig's ear, "Yesterday your master stopped my breath, and today I've stopped yours. Your master once wished that the mustard would bring me good luck, and now it has given me better luck than he ever imagined."

Gentlemen must be careful not to make sport and play tricks on poor men.

The True Origin of the Fish Called Old Maids or Young Maids

ONCE SOME HANDSOME YOUNG men were swimming in the sea, and some wanton ladies and girls arrived. They told the young men to come out and kiss them. But the youths would not come out. Consequently, the ladies stripped themselves and ran into the water after them. And the gentle young men were driven away and swam further into the water. The ladies followed them further until all were lost, boys and girls. As a result, the young men were changed into codfish because they were too shy of the girls who loved them, and the ladies were turned into old maids and young maids because they were too wanton and bad.

Men should not be too modest, nor the girls too forward.

The Spider

ONCE THERE WAS A girl, as there are many today, and she was a good needle-worker and could make a beautiful cloak in one day. Now, this girl loved a gentleman very much. However, one day her sweetheart was sent to prison, and when she heard it, she hastened and went to the king and begged him humbly to let her love go free. Well, the king promised her, if she would make him a fine cloak—one every day for a week, seven cloaks for seven days—he would forgive him and permit him to go free.

The young lady hastened to do it, and for six days she worked hard and cheerfully at it, and every evening she sent a cloak to the king. But one day she happened to become tired and did not wish to work because it was rainy, and she could not dry or bleach the cloth in the sunlight. Consequently, the king said that if she could not work seven days to get her lover, the gentleman must remain imprisoned, for she did not love him enough as she should. Then the maid became so angry and vexed in her heart that she died of grief and was changed into a spider. So it is that to this day she spreads out her threads when the sun shines, and the dewdrops, which you see on them, are the tears which she has wept for her lover.

If you remain idle one summer day you may lose a whole week's work, my dear. You say that you would like to hear more stories! All right. I will tell you a nice story. Remember all I tell you is what I've remembered from my grandfather.

Witchcraft

"MY DEAR AUNT, I wish very much to be a witch. I would like to enchant people and to know secret things. You can teach me all that."

"Oh, my darling! If you become a witch, and the Gentiles know it, you will have a good deal of trouble. All the children will cry aloud, and make a noise and throw stones at you when they see you, and perhaps the grown-up people will kill you. But it is nice to know secret things and pleasant for a poor old humble woman whom everyone spits upon to know how to do them evil and pay them for their cruelty. So, I *will* teach you something of witchcraft. Listen!

"When you want to tell a fortune, put all your heart into finding out what kind of a man or woman you have to deal with. Look sharply and focus your eyes, especially if it be a girl. When she is half-frightened, she will tell you much without knowing it. When you will have done this often, you will be able to twist many a silly girl like twine around your fingers. Soon your eyes will look like a snake's, and when you are angry, you will look like the old devil. Half the business, my dear, is to know how to please, flatter, and allure people. When a girl has anything unusual in her face, you must tell her that it signifies extraordinary luck. If she have red or yellow hair, tell her that is a true sign that she will have a lot of gold. When her eyebrows meet, that shows she will be united to many rich gentlemen. Tell her always, when you see a mole on her cheek or her forehead or anything, that it is a sign she will become a great lady. Never mind where it is on her body, tell her always that a mole or fleck is a sign of greatness. *Praise her.* If you see that she has small hands or feet, tell her about a gentleman who is wild about pretty feet, and how a pretty band brings more luck than a pretty face. Praising and petting and alluring and crying-up are half of fortune-telling. There is no girl and no man on the Lord's earth who is not proud and vain about something, and if you can find it out, you can get their money. If you can, pick up all the gossip about people."

"But, my aunt, that is all humbug. I would like to learn real witchcraft. Tell me if there are no real witches, and how they look."

"A real witch, my child, has eyes like a bird, the corner turned up like the point of a curved pointed knife. Many Jews and un-Christians have such eyes. And witches' hairs are drawn out from the roots and straight, and then curled at the ends. When Gentile witches have green eyes, they are the most to be dreaded.

"I will tell you something magical. When you find a pen or an iron nail, and then a piece of paper, you should write on it with the pen all you wish, and eat it, and your wish will be fulfilled. But you must write all in your own blood. If you find a great shell or an old pitcher by the sea, put it to your ear, and you will hear a noise. If you can, when the full moon shines, sit quite naked in her light and listen to it. Each night the noise will become more distinct, and then you will hear the fairies talking plainly enough. When you make a hole with a stone in a tomb go there night after night, and before long, you will hear what the dead are saying. Often they reveal where money is buried. You must take a stone and turn it around in the tomb until a hole is there.

"Now, I'll tell you something more witchly. Observe everything that swims on water, on rivers, or the sea. You will hear the water-spirits, who live in the water, speak to the earth's witches. If a man sees cloth on the water and gets it, that shows he will get a sweetheart; the cleaner and nicer the cloth, the better the maid. If you find a stick or rod on the water, that shows you will beat your enemy. A shoe or cup floating on the water means that you will soon be loved by your sweetheart. And yellow flowers floating on the water foretell gold, and white, silver, and red, love.

"When you find a key, that will bring you lots of luck. When you pick it up, utter a male or female name, and the person will become your own. Very lucky is a red string or ribbon. Keep it. It foretells happy love. Don't ever let this escape your soul, my child."

"No, aunt, never."

Bibliography

Charles Godfrey Leland

Books

Meister Karl's Sketch-Book. Philadelphia: Parry & MacMillan, 1855.

Pictures of Travel and Book Songs. Trans. Heinrich Heine. Philadelphia: Weik, 1855.

The Poetry and Mystery of Dreams. Philadelphia: E. H. Butler, 1856.

Sunshine in Thought. New York: George P. Putnam, 1863.

The Art of Conversation. New York: Carleton, 1864.

Mother Pitcher's Poems. Philadelphia: Frederick Leypoldt, 1864.

The German Mother Goose. Philadelphia: Frederick Leypoldt, 1864.

Memoirs of a Good-for-Nothing. (Joseph von Eichendorff.) Philadelphia: Frederick Leypoldt, 1866.

Hans Breitmann's Ballads. 1868. Philadelphia: Peterson & Brothers, 1969.

Hans Breitmann's Party with Other Ballads. Philadelphia: T. B. Peterson & Brothers, 1868.

The Music Lesson of Confucius. London: Trübner, 1872.

The English Gypsies. London: Trübner, 1873.

English Gypsy Songs. In collaboration with E. H. Palmer and Janet Tuckey. London: Trübner, 1875.

Johnnykin. London: Macmillan & Co., 1879.

The Minor Arts: Arts at Home Series. London: Macmillan, 1879.

The Gypsies. Boston: Houghton Mifflin, 1882.

The Algonquin Legends of New England. Boston: Houghton Mifflin, 1884.

Brand-New Ballads. London: Fun Office, 1885.

Practical Education. London: Whittaker, 1888.

Drawing and Designing. Chicago: Rand, McNally, 1889.

Gypsy Sorcery and Fortune-Telling. London: T. Fisher Unwin, 1891.

The Works of Heinrich Heine: Translated from the German. London: William Heinemann, 1891–93.

The Book of One Hundred Riddles of the Fairy Bellaria. London: T. Fisher Unwin, 1892.

Memoirs. 2 vols. London: William Heinemann, 1893.

Etruscan Roman Remains in Popular Tradition. London: T. Fisher Unwin, 1893.

Legends of Florence, Collected from the People and Retold. 2 vols. London: David Nutt, 1895–96.

A Manual of Mending and Repairing. London: Chatto & Windus, 1896.

Aradia; or, The Gospel of the Witches. London: David Nutt, 1899.

Have You a Strong Will? London: George Redway, 1899.

The Unpublished Legends of Virgil. London: Eliot Stock, 1901.

Kulóskap the Master and Other Algonkin Poems. In collaboration with John Dyneley Prince. New York: Funk & Wagnalls, 1902.

The Alternate Sex. London: Philip Wellby, 1902.

Criticism

Bradley, Sculley. "Hans Breitmann in England and America." *Colophon: A Book Collectors' Quarterly* 2 (1936): 65–81.

Comparetti, Domenico. *Virgilio nel Medio Evo*. Florence: La Nuova Italia Editrice, 1872.

———. *Vergil in the Middle Ages*. Trans. E. F. M. Benecke. Intro. Jan M. Ziolkowski. Princeton: Princeton University Press, 1997.

Dorson, Richard. *The British Folklorists*. Chicago: University of Chicago Press, 1968.

———. "American Folklorists in Britain." *Journal of the Folklore Institute* 7 (1970): 187–219.

Jackson, Joseph. *A Bibliography of the Works of Charles Godfrey Leland*. Philadelphia: Historical Society of Pennsylvania, 1923.

Jagendorf, Moritz. "Charles Godfrey Leland—Neglected Folklorist." *New York Folklore Quarterly* 19 (1963): 211–19.

Owen, Mary Alicia. *Voodoo Tales*. Introduction by Charles Godfrey Leland. Philadelphia: George W. Jacobs, 1893.

———. *Ole Rabbit's Plantation Stories as Told among the Negroes of the South West*. Introduction by Charles Godfrey Leland. Philadelphia: George W. Jacobs, 1898.

Parkhill, Thomas. *Weaving Ourselves into the Land: Charles Godfrey Leland, "Indians," and the Study of Native American Religions*. Albany: State University of New York Press, 1979.

———. "Of Glooskap's Birth, and of His Brother Malsum, the Wolf: The Story of Charles Godfrey Leland's 'Purely American Creation.'" *American Indian Culture and Research Journal* 16, no. 1 (1992): 45–69.

Pazzaglini, Mario, and Dina Pazzaglini, trans. *Aradia; or, The Gospel of the Witches: A New Translation* with additional material by Chas S. Clifton, Robert Mathiesen, and Robert E. Chartowich, foreword by Stewart Farrar. Blaine, WA: Phoenix, 1998.

Pennell, Elizabeth Robins. "Hans Breitmann." *Atlantic Monthly* 95 (1905): 154–68.

———. *Charles Godfrey Leland: A Biography*. 2 vols. Boston: Houghton Mifflin, 1906.

———. Introduction to *Hans Breitmann's Ballads*, v–xvii. Boston: Houghton Mifflin, 1914.

Smith, Ralph Carlisle. "Charles Godfrey Leland: The American Years, 1824–1869." PhD diss., University of New Mexico, 1961.

Thalmann, Marianne. "Hans Breitmann." *PMLA* 54, no. 2 (1939): 579–88.

Varesano, Angela-Marie Joanna. "Charles Godfrey Leland: The Eclectic Folklorist." PhD diss., University of Pennsylvania, 1979.

Wienker-Pieho, Sabine. "Charles Godfrey Leland and His Breitmann Ballads." In *Ballad Mediations: Folksongs Recovered, Represented, and Reimagined*, ed. Roger de Renwick and Sigrid Rieuwerts, 156–69. Trier: Wissenschaftlicher, 2006.

Wood, Juliette. "Gipsy Witches and Celtic Magicians: Charles Godfrey Leland and Lewis Spence." *Béaloideas* 76 (2008): 1–22.

Zumwalt, Rosemary Lévy. *American Folklore Scholarship: A Dialogue of Dissent*. Bloomington: Indiana University Press, 1988.

Acknowledgments

Thanks to a research grant from the University of Minnesota Retirees Association I was able to examine and make great use of Charles Godfrey Leland's papers at the Library of Congress in Washington, D.C. In addition, I have benefited greatly from all the excellent scholarship on Leland listed in the bibliography. Most important, I should like to thank Annie Martin and Marie Sweetman, who have supported my work at Wayne State University Press, and Jennifer Backer, who has edited my manuscript with great care and insight. In addition, I am grateful for the careful work that Kristin Harpster and Emily Nowak have contributed to this book. Finally, I should like to dedicate this book to my wife, Carol Dines, who is the Bellaria in my life.

www.ingramcontent.com/pod-product-compliance
Lightning Source LLC
Chambersburg PA
CBHW051108030726
47504CB00006B/1837